and lifted her face for his kiss. It was gentle, unhurried, but with an undercurrent of leashed passion.

"I'm proud of you," David murmured. "I'd give anything if you weren't an actress, but I want you to be happy, and if this is what you want, then I wish you every success."

They were totally unaware of the crowds that swirled around them as Robyn's fingers carressed the back of David's blond head. "All I need to be happy is for you to hold me the way you're doing now," she answered honestly. "And if you'll kiss me I'll be even happier."

He caught his breath and stiffened, his face unreadable. "If you mean that, then come home with me—now."

PHYLLIS HALLDORSON,
like all her heroines, is as in love with her husband today as on the day they met. It is because she has known so much love in her own life that her characters seem to come alive as they, too, discover the joys of romance.

Dear Reader:

I'd like to take this opportunity to thank you for all your support and encouragement of Silhouette Romances.

Many of you write in regularly, telling us what you like best about Silhouette, which authors are your favorites. This is a tremendous help to us as we strive to publish the best contemporary romances possible.

All the romances from Silhouette Books are for you, so enjoy this book and the many stories to come. I hope you'll continue to share your thoughts with us, and invite you to write to us at the address below:

Karen Solem
Editor-in-Chief
Silhouette Books
P.O. Box 769
New York, N.Y. 10019

PHYLLIS HALLDORSON
Mountain Melody

Silhouette Romance

Published by Silhouette Books New York

America's Publisher of Contemporary Romance

Other Silhouette Books by Phyllis Halldorson

Temporary Bride
To Start Again

SILHOUETTE BOOKS, a Division of Simon & Schuster, Inc.
1230 Avenue of the Americas, New York, N.Y. 10020

Copyright © 1983 by Phyllis Halldorson

Distributed by Pocket Books

ISBN: 0-671-57247-4

First Silhouette Books printing September, 1983

10 9 8 7 6 5 4 3 2 1

Map by Ray Lundgren

America's Publisher of Contemporary Romance

Printed in the U.S.A.
BC91

For Jiggs,
who taught my heart to sing.

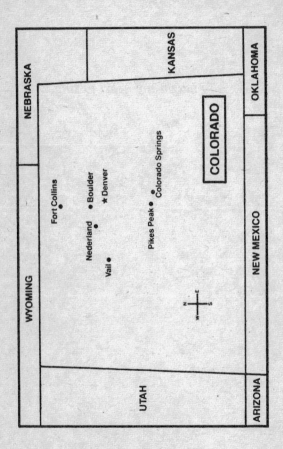

Chapter One

Robyn seethed as she scrubbed at the front of the clinging, low-cut electric-blue jump suit, which matched her eyes. The outfit was new, and she'd only worn it to the cocktail party because her roommate at the boarding house in Boulder had taken a fancy to it and urged her to.

"Come on, Robyn," she'd said, "you've never met most of the cast and crew you'll be working with this summer, so wear something that will grab their attention. Besides, Lowell St. James, the drama critic for the Denver newspaper, is supposed to be there, and you'll want him to notice you. You don't always want to be known as just a member of the chorus, do you?"

Robyn held the washcloth under the cold-water tap, wrung it out and again attacked the large wet spot on her bosom. It didn't look as if it was going to stain, but the fumes were overpowering. Darn it! Why did that clod with two left feet have to stumble over one of them and pour his whiskey sour down her neck? She smelled like a distillery!

Robyn didn't like cocktail parties, never had and probably never would. She'd only come to this one because it was a command performance given by the producer of the new summer program of musical comedies. They were going to be performed under a mammoth tent on a round stage in the center of a shallow pit with the audience seated all around it. It was called theater-in-the-round, and Robyn was eagerly looking forward to the start of rehearsals in a few days.

Most of the crew and part of the cast were local people, but some, like Robyn, had been brought in. Actually, she supposed she could be considered local since she'd been born and raised in nearby Greeley and had graduated with a degree in fine arts from the University of Colorado at Boulder a year before. Since then, though, she'd been touring with a national company of a hit Broadway musical. It was a marvelous opportunity even though she was only a member of the chorus, and she was being considered for a part in the show they were planning for the following year. Meanwhile, during the summer, she'd auditioned for and been accepted by this smaller but more versatile company. It would be a relief to stay in one place for three months!

Someone banged on the bathroom door, and Robyn sighed and dried herself off as best as she could. Now she'd have to go home, which would certainly not be any great hardship.

The party had been a bore from the beginning, and why they'd decided to hold it at Nederland, about twenty miles up the mountain from Boulder, where they were all staying, was a mystery. Someone had said the host was a wealthy patron of the arts who wanted to show off his newly renovated Victorian show place of a home.

The banging on the door began again, and Robyn quickly hung up the towel and walked out of the bathroom, intent on leaving immediately.

Like most Victorian homes, this one had plenty of rooms, but they were all fairly small. With fifty or more people mingling around and most of them a little tipsy, it was fast becoming a madhouse.

As she tried to remember which way was the front door, Robyn wondered if the drama critic from Denver had shown up. There had been a lot of introductions this afternoon, but since they were all strangers to her, it was impossible to remember what face went with which name. However, she was sure she would have remembered Lowell St. James.

As she nudged her way through the crowded rooms, Robyn opened her purse and pulled out her soft brocade glasses case. She was nearsighted and usually wore contact lenses, but one of her eyes had been slightly inflamed that morning, so she'd worn her large shell-rimmed glasses instead. She'd taken them off during the party—it really wasn't necessary to see across the room—but she couldn't drive without them.

She carefully removed the glasses from the case and was trying to maneuver them onto her nose with one hand while she put the case back in her purse with the other when someone bumped against her arm and the frames slipped from her fingers and fell to the floor. Before she could reach for them, a large black boot crushed them underneath and walked on.

"Oh, no!" Robyn moaned as she retrieved the

splintered lenses. Now what was she going to do? It said on her driver's license that she was supposed to wear corrective lenses when she drove. She'd just have to drive carefully and hope she wasn't stopped by a patrolman.

In her haste to get away before anything else happened, she forcefully pushed open the front screen door, almost slamming it into a man standing just outside on the porch. He was of average size with brown hair and eyes, and she murmured a hasty apology as she brushed past him.

Before she made it to the porch steps, Robyn realized she was in for still more trouble. Sometime in the past couple of hours, a storm had moved in and thunder, which couldn't be heard in the noisy house, was rumbling overhead. A breeze had sprung up, and heavy black rain clouds left the area in near darkness, although it was only seven o'clock on a late June evening.

Her heart sank as she moved quickly down the steps and along the sidewalk to where she had parked her red Pinto. It was bad enough that she had to drive without her glasses, but the stormy darkness made it even worse. She'd always had trouble seeing at night. Her mother called it "night blindness" and said it ran in the family.

Robyn was fumbling in her purse for the keys to her car when a gravely male voice from behind startled her. "Excuse me, honey, are you going back to Boulder?"

She turned to see the man she'd nearly run into on the porch. He must have followed her.

"Yes," she answered, "I am."

"Look, I'm in a bind," he began. "My bird-brained wife dropped me off here and went on to visit her sister, who has a summer cabin just off the Boulder Canyon road. She was supposed to pick me up no later than six-thirty, but as usual, she's late, and I've got to be in Boulder in half an hour for a very important appointment. How about giving me a ride as far as my sister-in-law's cabin? It's not out of your way, and I've got to keep that appointment."

He sounded a little desperate, and there was also an undertone of anger in his voice. Robyn decided she'd hate to be his wife when he finally caught up with her.

She hesitated as she fitted her key in the lock, playing for time. After all, this man was a stranger; she'd never seen him before—at least if he'd been in the house, she didn't remember seeing him. On the other hand, he was obviously a guest at the party, which meant he was also a member of the show troupe, in which case it wouldn't be very nice of her to refuse to help him out.

There was a flash of lightning as she opened the door and turned toward him. He looked at her anxiously as he said, "Sorry, I didn't introduce myself. My name is—"

A clap of thunder drowned out his voice, and suddenly the skies opened up, and the rain poured down. It was too late now for formalities—they were quickly getting drenched.

Robyn raised her voice so she could be heard above the wind and rain. "Do you drive?"

He nodded. "Yes."

Maybe he was sent in answer to her prayers, Robyn thought. He could drive as far as his sister-in-law's cabin, and hopefully by then the storm would have abated. She slid across the seat to the passenger side of the car and held out the keys to him as he settled behind the steering wheel.

As he started the motor, Robyn reached for the seat belt and tugged. Nothing happened. She tugged again, but it was apparently jammed. Then she remembered that the last passenger she'd had—it must have been two weeks ago—had mentioned the seat belt wasn't working. She'd intended to have it fixed but then forgot about it since she never rode on the passenger side. Well, there was nothing she could do about it now, but she made a mental note to have it fixed first thing Monday.

By the time they turned onto the highway, Robyn knew she'd made a mistake. The man was angrier than she'd thought, and he was driving much too fast. Thank heavens there wasn't much traffic, but with the wet road and the rain coming down so heavily that the windshield wipers couldn't keep up with it, he was taking dangerous chances.

She braced her hands against the dashboard and said, "You're going too fast. Please slow down a little."

He stared straight ahead and muttered, "Been driving for thirty years and never had an accident. Got a deadline to meet. Watch for an access road on the left. Damn! I can't see a thing."

His foot pressed down farther on the gas pedal, and Robyn stiffened in her seat, wondering what she could say or do that would make the man slow down without making him madder. He'd been drinking more than she'd realized and wasn't altogether rational. God, how could she have been so stupid to pick up a stranger?

A jagged streak of lightning lit the sky, and Robyn saw a dirt road leading up the side of the canyon just ahead. "There's a road," she shouted over the noise of the thunder. With a squeal of brakes, the man veered the car off the highway, almost missing the narrow road that wound upward through a forest of lodgepole pine.

They continued up and around at a fast pace. What little light they'd had before was now cut off by the towering trees, and the landscape was a blur to Robyn. She braced herself against the seat, afraid that at any minute they would miss a turn and hit a tree. Why did that seat belt have to malfunction now?

Bolts of lightning zigzagged to earth, and in the eerie light, a large summer home, set back in a clearing surrounded by trees, came into view up ahead. Robyn trembled with relief. Oh, thank God, this must be the place the man was looking for!

Just as she started to relax, a small figure bolted into the headlights several yards ahead of them. It was a child running across the road! Robyn screamed, and the man stomped on the brakes. They screeched in protest as the back wheels locked, and the car skidded crazily along the slippery road. Robyn heard a soft thud near the right fender before her head hit the dashboard and red pain exploded behind her eyes.

At first, Robyn couldn't identify the noise, but then she realized it was voices, men's and women's, shouting at each other against the background rhythm of the rainfall. Her face was pushed against a rod of some sort with open spaces on either side. She opened her eyes and turned her head slightly, then winced as a wave of pain made her gasp.

She was lying across the steering wheel, and the car was stopped, but the windshield wipers were still working. Back and forth, back and forth, like a lullaby lulling her to sleep. If only that commotion outside would stop. What were those people yelling about . . . ?

When she awakened again, a man's voice in the distance was barking orders. "Eve, call the highway patrol and tell them to send an ambulance immediately! Graham, come here with that flashlight. Now that we've gotten Shelley in the house, I'll see what shape that maniac of a driver is in."

The door beside her was jerked open, and a large pair of hands clamped around her shoulders and carefully lifted her off the steering wheel. She cried out as waves of agony coursed through her, and the hands settled her back against the seat.

Robyn opened her eyes and by the dim car light saw the face of the man bending over her. It would have been a handsome face if it hadn't been so pale and twisted into such a fierce scowl. No, not a scowl exactly, more like a combination of anguish and terror. Jade-green eyes bored into her, and Robyn shivered.

Another male voice spoke from behind the first man. "Is she all right, David?"

The man called David was running his hands over her face, shoulders, arms, ribs, hips, legs. She knew she should stop him, but she couldn't move or speak, and he wasn't being the least offensive. His hands were gentle but firm, and she realized he was examining her for broken bones. Maybe he was a doctor.

Apparently satisfied that nothing was broken, David moved her right eyelid up and beamed a light straight into her eye, then did the same with the left one. She tried to jerk her head away, but it hurt to move.

Finally, he called over his shoulder to the man behind, "I can't detect any broken bones, and her eyes focus okay. Hell, she's too pickled in booze to get hurt; the car reeks of whiskey. That's what usually happens; the innocent victim gets killed, and the drunk behind the wheel gets off without a scratch. By God, I'll see she rots in prison if Shelley—"

He choked on what sounded like a sob, and Robyn cringed at the bitterness in his voice.

Then his words penetrated the fog that had clouded her mind. *Innocent victim killed. Shelley.*

The child! Oh, good Lord, the car had hit the child!

She tried to sit up, but the man pushed her back and ordered, "Lie still. We'll have you out of here in a minute."

"The child?" She had trouble mouthing the words. "What about—the child?"

"How kind of you to be concerned." His voice was heavy with sarcasm. "She's alive," he snapped, "but I don't know for how long."

A cry of remorse rose from her throat and mingled with the sound of the rain. David unfastened her seat belt and slid his arms under her, then lifted her carefully and started to the house. Robyn wound her arms around his neck and buried her face against his wet shirt as the sobs that shook her were drowned out by the sounds of the storm.

Inside the house, David dumped her on a couch and told her to stay there, then disappeared. There was no chance to ask questions even if she'd been able to form them in the muddle of her mind. She was wet and trembling, and for a long time she sobbed, unable to control the spasms that shook her. She could hear people running around and voices in another part of the house, but nobody came into the small room where she lay.

Finally, the convulsive shudders subsided, and Robyn sank back into the cushions, exhausted. How was the child? Where was she? It must be a girl for the man had called her Shelley. How old was she, and how badly was she hurt? And where was the man who had been driving? Was he hurt, too? She couldn't remember seeing him or hearing anything about him in all the confusion.

Her head throbbed, and she felt nauseated. Maybe if she closed her eyes for a little while . . .

The next time Robyn awoke, there was a woman standing beside the couch where she lay. She was middle-aged, short and round with gray-streaked brown hair pulled back from her face in a bun at the back of her head. She wore an apron over her print cotton dress, and her faded blue eyes were red-rimmed in her pale, pinched face.

The woman was obviously in great distress, and Robyn's first thought was of the child, the little girl who had been hit by the car.

Her voice wavered as she tried to speak. "The child, Shel—Shelley. How is she?" Somewhere on the rim of her subconscious, she remembered someone barking orders to call an ambulance. "Did the ambulance come? Has she been taken to the hospital?"

The woman's eyes clouded with tears, and her lips trembled as she fought to keep her voice steady. "The telephone lines were knocked out by the storm, so we can't get through to an ambulance service. Her father got in the car and started for Nederland to get help, but there's been a rock slide across the private road that comes up here. He couldn't get around it and had to come back."

Robyn started shivering again. "Oh, no," she cried. "But Shelley, is she badly hurt?"

The woman's face became hard, cold. "She has a broken leg and a deep cut on her elbow where it broke the headlight on your car. Dr. David set her leg and sewed up her arm, but he thinks there may be internal bleeding. He's desperate to get her to a hospital."

Robyn pushed herself up to a sitting position fighting nausea and the wave of dizziness that blurred her vision. "Her father is a physician?"

"A veterinarian," the woman replied. "The best in the area, but little girls are different than puppies and besides, he can't do much without tests and X-rays."

She abruptly switched the topic of conversation. "I'm Dr. David's housekeeper, Irene Skinner. He told me to see that you had a hot bath and some dry clothes. You'll catch pneumonia in those wet things. Can you walk?"

Robyn's head had cleared, and she nodded. "I think so. Mrs. Skinner, what happened to the man?"

The housekeeper had already turned and started out of the room. "Call me Irene," she said. "Everyone does. What man?"

She didn't wait for a reply but called, "Follow me," over her shoulder and walked away.

"The man who was driving my car," Robyn said as she tottered across a hall, through a living room, and started up a staircase, trying to keep up with the rapidly disappearing Irene and not collapse. She could hear voices again coming from various parts of the house but saw no one.

The housekeeper apparently didn't hear her. She beckoned to Robyn to follow her through a doorway that led into a large bedroom that seemed somewhat overcrowded with furniture. "Get out of those wet clothes while I run your bath," she ordered as she opened a door that led into a bathroom.

The water was hot and steamy and filled with bubbles, and after soaking in its delicious warmth for a while, Robyn finally stopped shivering, although she was still hazy and nauseated. She realized she must be suffering from shock; that was also Irene's diagnosis as she helped Robyn into the bathtub over Robyn's embarrassed protests. "Dr. David said I wasn't to leave you alone while you were in the bath, and I always follow his orders."

Irene left the door open between the bathroom and the bedroom as she gathered up Robyn's wet clothes off the floor where she'd stepped out of them and dumped them into the wash basin. She ran water, added soap and proceeded to wash the soiled jump suit and the lacy bits of underwear, grumbling as she worked. "I'll have to borrow something from Miss Joyce for you to wear. She's about your size. Miss Eve's too tall and skinny. You'd never fit into her things. Those fashion models look like skeletons with skin stretched over them."

Robyn lathered her arms with fragrant soap and said, "Who are Joyce and Eve?"

Irene ran the soapy water out of the basin and added clear rinse water. "Eve is Mrs. Graham Welles. She and her husband live next door to Dr. David in Boulder and are houseguests this week, and Joyce Fredericks is her younger sister. She's staying here, too. Got her eye set on Dr. David. Humph. Little good it'll do her, what with him moping over his ex-wife."

Robyn gathered from Irene's uninhibited conversation that "Dr. David" owned this house, had a daughter Shelley, a divorced wife, presumably Shelley's mother, and three houseguests, one of whom was his current girl friend. She smiled and wondered if "Dr. David" knew how few secrets he had.

Irene wrapped a soft yellow bath towel around Robyn sarong style and insisted that she sit on the side of the bed while she went in search of something for Robyn to wear. As soon as Irene was out of the room, Robyn stood up and approached the massive dark-wood dresser, backed by a matching wall mirror.

She had no idea where her purse was, but there was a sterling silver men's hairbursh on the highly polished dresser, and she picked it up and ran it through her thick auburn hair. The face that looked back at her from the mirror was an unpleasant surprise. There was a large purple bruise across one side of her forehead that extended part way down her cheek and disappeared into her hair. She also had the beginning of a black eye.

So that's why her head hurt! She'd sustained a hard blow. That would also account for her grogginess and the persistent nausea.

She put down the brush and looked around her. No wonder the room had seemed crowded. Not only did it contain the massive dresser, but there was also a large leather chair, a smaller velvet one and two double beds with a night table and a brass lamp between them. Two double beds? That was an odd arrangement. Was it possible that two couples slept in here at the same time? She shrugged. Sounded a little kinky, but everyone to his own taste.

She heard someone coming and just made it to the

bed closest to the door when Irene walked in with a cream-colored piece of satin over her arm. She handed it to Robyn and said, "Here's a nightgown. Put it on. Miss Joyce wasn't too happy to part with it, so be careful you don't damage it." She started back out of the room. "Dr. David wants to talk to you. I told him to wait five minutes, so you'd better get into that nightie and under the covers."

That's exactly where Robyn was five minutes later—propped up with pillows in the middle of the bed, the brown, gold and green plaid sheet pulled up under her arms to conceal the revealing lace bodice of the borrowed gown—when a knock sounded on the door. Before she could answer, the door opened, and Robyn recognized the man who had examined her in the car, then carried her into the house.

He leaned against the closed door and studied her, the rich auburn hair that curled against her white, slender shoulders, the one indigo eye and the one black eye. He was dressed in blue jeans, a sweatshirt and boots, and Robyn had never seen such a cold look of utter disgust on anyone's face before. She cringed against the pillows, as though his antagonism was palpable, but couldn't look away.

David was tall, over six feet, and built like an athlete, with wide shoulders and a slender waist and hips. His blond hair was tousled, as though he hadn't taken the time to comb it since he'd been out in the rain, and his green eyes looked bruised with shock and pain. Judging by his physique, Robyn would have thought he was in his twenties, but the lines of suffering on his face made him look much older. He was probably in his middle thirties.

He didn't move as he began to speak. "I'm David Christopher. Irene says you're able to function normally. How are you feeling?"

His voice sounded cordial enough, but she could sense the pent-up violence behind it. "I—I'm all right. How's your little girl?"

He stiffened and walked toward the bed. "She's got a broken left leg and a deep laceration on her left elbow. I can't be sure about other injuries until we can get her to a hospital, which may not be for quite some time."

He stood by the bed and explored the bruise on her head and cheek with his long fingers. She winced with pain, and he took a small light from his shirt pocket and once again used it to examine her eyes. Apparently satisfied, he put it back in his pocket and growled, "Who are you, and what were you doing speeding along on this private road in an electrical storm?"

He no longer sounded cordial, and the violence was showing through. Robyn bit her lip and answered, "We—we must have taken the wrong turnoff. It was raining—"

"We?" How could one little word sound so scornful? "What do you mean, 'we'?"

"The—the person who was with me. The man who was driving my car. He—"

The look of murderous rage that flitted across David's face stopped her. The promise of violence in his voice broke through, clear and unblemished, as he thundered, "No way, lady! I wondered what kind of an alibi you'd come up with, but I gave you credit for inventing a better one than that. Don't give me that hurt and frightened little girl look. If you're trying to tell me you weren't driving the car, forget it! You were belted in behind the steering wheel, reeking of liquor, and there wasn't another person in sight or any sign that there had been anyone else in that car."

His fingers flexed as though itching to clamp around her throat. "You drunken little fool, you hit my daughter! If she's maimed, I'm going to use every bit of influence I have to lock you away for the rest of your life!"

Chapter Two

David abruptly turned his back on Robyn and moved across the room to the window. For a moment, the only sound was the rain beating against the glass and pouring down on the corrugated metal roof.

Robyn could only stare, stunned by David's words and the enmity with which they were spoken. A flash of lightning momentarily lit up the darkness outside the window, and she could see the trees bending in the wind. The resulting roar of thunder seemed to shake the house and also roused her from her shocked daze.

Her voice was low, incredulous, as she spoke to David's back. "You can't mean that! There was a man with me. He was driving because I'd broken my glasses. He slammed on the brake, but the car skidded—"

David turned around, and his look was filled with disgust. "You're not going to lie your way out of this. Tell me, who was this supposed man?"

Robyn shook her head. "I don't know. I—"

His eyebrows raised inquiringly. "Don't know?"

"No," she said. "We were both guests at a cocktail

party in Nederland, and he needed a ride to his sister-in-law's cabin. I let him drive because I don't see well—"

"What's his name?" he cut in harshly.

"I—I don't know."

"Oh?" Again, the raised eyebrow. "Are you in the habit of picking up strange men at cocktail parties and not even asking their names?"

"No! You're making it sound awful. Please, just let me tell you," she pleaded.

He said nothing, and she continued. "This man told me that his wife was supposed to pick him up at six-thirty but she was late and he had an important appointment. He asked if I would take him to where his wife was, a cabin somewhere in Boulder Canyon. I swear he was driving. I asked him to slow down, but he wouldn't."

"What were you doing on this road?" he snarled. "It ends right here. There are no other cabins anywhere near, and I assure you the only married woman here has her husband with her."

Robyn hung her head. "I don't know." She sighed. "He didn't seem to know exactly where the turnoff was. He must have gotten the wrong road."

David snorted impatiently and began to pace. "How very convenient, but there are too many holes in your story, doll. You'll never make it stick. Oh, I can believe you were on your way to an assignation with a strange man at a cabin around here, but don't try to tell me he was with you. You were on your way to him, weren't you, but you took the wrong road. *You* were drunk and speeding and couldn't stop when you saw Shelley, although the skid marks indicate that you were far enough away when you applied the brakes that you could have missed her if you'd been traveling at even a reasonable rate of speed."

"No! No! No!" Robyn screamed. She could feel hysteria rising and fought to keep it under control. She made an effort to lower her voice as she continued. "I wasn't drunk. I'd only had two Tom Collins in three hours, and I'd munched on finger food with them. I never drink much. I don't even particularly like liquor."

"How sweet," he murmured dryly. "A real little virginal innocent, aren't you? Only it won't play." His tone became menacing as his voice escalated in volume. "The odor of whiskey around you was sickening. I was the first one there. I smelled it. So did Graham. You were bombed out of your mind, and if I just had some way of doing a blood test, I'd prove it beyond any doubt."

"No!" Robyn was sobbing again. How could she get through to this man who was determined to think the worst of her? It all sounded so plausible the way he told it. What on earth had become of the stranger who caused all this? How could he have just disappeared after the crash?

She struggled to keep her voice steady as tears streamed down her bruised face. "I can explain the whiskey smell. I never drink it—I can't stand the taste—but some clumsy oaf at the party tripped and spilled a highball glass full of it down the front of me. You're right. I did smell like a distillery, but it wasn't *in* me. It was *on* me."

For a moment, he looked uncertain. "Then you won't mind producing the garment in question so I can see for myself?"

"Of course," she answered eagerly, then remembered. She bit her lip and looked away. "I'm sorry, I can't," she murmured. "Your housekeeper has already washed it out." She felt sick with regret.

David pounded his fist against his hand and swore. "Will you stop making up these ridiculous lies!" he roared. "You don't even do it well. I'd advise you to tell the truth. It doesn't make any difference to me, but you might gain some points with the district attorney if you throw yourself on his mercy. You're an awfully tempting little package, and he is, after all, a man."

David's gaze slid to her bosom, and Robyn realized that sometime during the argument she'd let the sheet slip from her fingers, exposing her full breasts, which were barely covered by the lacy bodice of the low-cut nightgown.

She grabbed the sheet and again covered herself as a loud knock on the door was followed by a man's voice. "David, are you in there?"

David muttered an oath of annoyance and answered, "Come in, Graham."

The door opened, and a dark-haired man of medium height with blue eyes and a worried frown walked in. He looked at David. "What's going on in here? We could hear you all the way to Shelley's room. Look, David, as your lawyer, I must warn you, don't browbeat this girl. You could get the whole case thrown out of court later on—"

"Browbeat, hell!" David shouted. "I'm just trying to find out what she was doing up here. This is a private road. She had no business—"

The man put his hand on David's arm. "Come on, pal, calm down. Get out of here now and let the young lady rest." He turned to look at Robyn, and his eyes opened wide with surprise. "You didn't tell me she had a head injury."

Robyn watched apprehensively as he approached the bed where she lay. Like David, this man was wearing blue jeans and a sweatshirt, but instead of boots, he wore soft leather house slippers on his feet.

He stood looking down at her. "I'm Graham Welles, Dr. Christopher's friend, next-door neighbor and attorney. Do you feel up to answering a few questions?"

Robyn knew this had to be gotten through sooner or later, and she decided it better be sooner. She nodded, and Graham motioned David to sit down, then perched himself on the side of the bed.

David sat on the edge of the other bed, and Graham started the inquisition. "Will you please tell me your name and address and the name of your insurance company?"

"My name is Robyn Elizabeth Flannery," she said, "and I've only just come to Boulder. I'm staying in a boarding house, but my parents live in Greeley, and I was born and raised there."

She gave him her address in Boulder, her parents' address in Greeley and the name of her insurance company but explained that her card was in her purse and she hadn't seen her purse since the accident.

He was writing her answers down in a small leather note pad he'd taken from his pocket. "How old are you, Robyn?"

She leaned back and closed her eyes. Her head was throbbing, and she felt a little dizzy. "I'm twenty-three, and I graduated last year from the university at Boulder with a degree in fine arts."

"Are you an artist?" David asked.

"No, I—"

"She's in no condition to be questioned further, David," Graham interrupted as he closed his notebook and stood up. "Go to sleep now. We'll go over this more thoroughly in the morning when you're feeling better. By the way, how did you get up here? The road has been closed by a rock slide."

"It wasn't when we went over it," Robyn murmured drowsily.

"We?" Graham's interest picked up.

"Never mind, Graham," David said. "I'll tell you all about it."

The two men left, and Robyn snuggled into the soft bed, falling asleep instantly.

The first thing Robyn noticed when she awoke was that the rain had let up. It was still coming down, but more gently now.

It was very dark, and her lighted digital watch read three o'clock. She'd slept soundly and felt better. The headache was gone, and she was thirsty.

She turned on the lamp on the night table and headed for the bathroom. The water was cool and refreshing as it slid down her parched throat. There was a stale taste in her mouth, so she gargled with a mint-flavored mouthwash she found in the medicine cabinet. A glance in the mirror showed that the bruise on her head and cheek was even darker and more pronounced and the hint of a black eye was no longer a hint. She looked as if she'd gone ten rounds in a boxing ring!

Robyn turned off the light in the bathroom and returned to the bedroom. The house was quiet, the only sound the tap, tap, tap of rain on the roof. She sat on the edge of the bed, wondering how the child was. No one had mentioned how old she was, and the glimpse Robyn had had of her in the headlights was too fleeting to be more than an impression.

What on earth had the little girl been doing outside in the stormy darkness? She'd been running—Robyn was sure of that—but why? At the height of an electrical storm, what could drive her out into the night?

Robyn remembered how afraid she'd been of electrical storms as a child. Nothing would have induced her to go out in one. At the first sound of thunder, she would run to her mother and cuddle in her warm, protective embrace.

But Shelley apparently didn't have a mother to run to. Her father and mother were divorced, and at least for now, she was with her father. Where was her mother? What would she do when she found out her daughter had been injured? Would she blame David for not watching her more closely? Maybe she should, because it was odd that with at least five adults in the house, the child would be running around outside in a violent storm with no one apparently paying any attention.

Robyn shivered and rubbed her hands down her arms. It was chilly, but she didn't have a robe to put on. Irene had hung her clothes on the shower-curtain rod, but they were still damp, and the skimpy nightie was no protection at all.

She knew she should get back into bed, but she suddenly had to find out how Shelley was. If she wandered around the house, she could at least find out if the youngster was restless and in pain or if she was sleeping peacefully.

Robyn opened the bedroom door and stepped out into the hall. It was dark, but at the other end of the corridor, there was a dim light shining through the open door of a room. That must be where Shelley was.

She walked quietly, her bare feet making no sound on the carpeted floor, until she reached the lighted room. Inside, she saw a child lying on a maple colonial-style bed; beside it, David sat dozing and looking uncomfortable in an upholstered armchair.

Robyn tiptoed across the room and looked down at the slender, curly-headed girl whose left leg was splinted and propped up on pillows. Her little face was white and pinched, and her open gray-green eyes were clouded, probably from the painkiller she'd been given.

Robyn's heart lurched as she tried to force her mouth into a smile. "Hi," she said softly. "I'm Robyn. How do you feel?"

The girl looked Robyn over carefully, then said, "I hurt."

Oh, the poor little thing, Robyn thought. She looked so small and battered and miserable lying there with her leg at an uncomfortable angle and her left arm in a sling. Her honey-colored hair was a mass of muddy tangles on the pink pillow, and her pale cheeks were streaked with dried tears.

"Can I get you anything?" Robyn asked.

For a minute, Shelley didn't answer; then she spoke hesitantly. "Will you get me a drink of water?"

She motioned toward the table at the bedside, and Robyn saw a container of ice water and a glass with a straw. She poured water in the glass and held it low so the child could sip it through the straw.

Shelley took several swallows and then turned her head away. Robyn set the glass back on the table, then picked up a nursery-size straight-backed chair and put it close to the bed, being careful not to awaken the man sleeping in the chair on the other side. He looked exhausted and tense even in repose. She felt the stirring of compassion. It must have been a horrendous shock for him to hear the scream of brakes and find his daughter crumpled beside a damaged car in the road.

David shifted and groaned sleepily as he settled into a more comfortable position. Not that any position would be comfortable for his long, lean body in that totally inadequate chair, Robyn thought. He'd turned his face into the dim glow from the small night light, and she studied his rugged features. His face was long but not narrow, and deep lines ran from the edges of his nostrils around the corners of his mouth. She knew that if he ever smiled, his wide mouth would deepen the lines even more. His straight blond hair fell in disarray over his broad forehead, but his eyelashes were dark and thick and almost long enough to touch his cheek when they were closed over his green eyes.

Robyn shifted her gaze away from him and back to Shelley, who was watching her, puzzled. "Are you a friend of my daddy's?" she asked.

Robyn hesitated. She wasn't going to lie to this child, who'd learn the truth eventually, anyway. "No, Shelley, I'm not. It was my car that hit you."

Shelley's eyes widened. "Oh."

She said nothing more, and finally Robyn broke the silence. She brushed a tangled curl away from the none-too-clean forehead and asked, "How old are you?"

"Eight. But I'm going on nine," Shelley explained seriously. "How old are you?"

Well, I laid myself wide open for that, Robyn

thought as she said, "I'm twenty-three going on twenty-two."

The corners of the little girl's mouth turned up in a small grin. "You can't do that. That's going backwards."

Robyn pretended surprise. "Really? Well look, I won't tell anyone if you don't."

Shelley laughed, erasing the taut, pained expression and revealing delicate, symmetrical features that held a promise of beauty.

Robyn took the small hand that lay on top of the cover and murmured quietly, "You'd better go back to sleep."

Shelley's eyes searched her face. "Will you stay with me?"

Robyn nodded. "If you want me to. Would you like for me to sing to you?"

"Can you sing?" Shelley asked.

Robyn smiled. "A little. How about this?"

Her warm, vibrant contralto voice wafted softly through the room as she sang the opening notes of Brahms' Lullaby, followed by "Rock-a-Bye-Baby." She continued to hum gently after the translucent eyelids had closed over Shelley's gray-green eyes and the little hand had relaxed its grip until she was sure the sleeping child would not waken again.

She carefully tucked the covers around Shelley and stood, her muscles cramped from her awkward position by the bed. She stretched to relieve the tautness, and as she did so, she turned slightly and found herself looking straight into the quizzical green eyes of Shelley's father, David Christopher.

For just a moment those eyes were filled with a surprised approval, but with a flicker of an eyelash, it was gone, replaced by the harsh, cold censure that had been there earlier.

David sat up and rubbed his hands over his face, but when he spoke, the anger was still there. "What are you doing in here Miss—Miss—"

"Robyn Flannery," she reminded him, "and I came to see how Shelley was. Please, I just got her to sleep. Don't waken her."

He glanced at his sleeping daughter. "I heard you. Now I want you to hear me, and hear me good." There was grim menace in his voice as he continued. "Stay away from Shelley! If you think that by playing up to her, letting her think you're her friend, you can persuade me not to prosecute you for reckless drunk driving, you are very much mistaken."

He glared at her. "That's a despicable thing to do, deliberately encouraging a child's love and trust for your own gain, and I won't stand for it."

Robyn stood gaping at him, unable for a moment to believe what he was saying. How on earth had he ever come up with such a monstrous idea? "I'm not!" she squealed before she remembered to lower her voice. "I only wanted to find out how she was, and when I got here, she was awake and asked for a drink of water."

"I was here to look after her," he grated.

"You were asleep," she pointed out reasonably.

He looked away. "Yes, well—I would have heard her if she'd called."

"Of course you would have," Robyn agreed, "but you need rest, too. Why don't you let me sit with her while you go to bed and get some sleep?"

His gaze wandered slowly, suggestively, over her slender but nicely rounded figure, lingering on the bare white shoulders, the partially exposed breasts and the tiny waist encased in the clinging nightgown. She felt a hot flush of embarrassment as she realized the cream-colored satin of the skirt revealed almost as much as it covered, but she stood still under his scrutiny, determined not to respond to his baiting.

"You fill out Joyce's nightgown in a most provocative manner," he said, ignoring her suggestion.

Robyn felt a stab of resentment, not so much because of his disrespectful manner but because he'd known without being told that the nightgown she was wearing belonged to Joyce. Well, why wouldn't he? If she was his current girl friend, he'd probably taken it off her enough times to recognize it.

David's eyes moved up the slender column of her throat, past the set, determined chin and full pink lips to her bruised cheek and forehead, partially covered by a fall of auburn hair.

"Maybe I was wrong about you," he mused as he stood and stretched slowly. "Could it be *me* you're trying to seduce? Are you offering me a night of 'forbidden delights' in exchange for not being charged with a crime?"

Robyn jerked as though he had slapped her, and she could feel the blood draining from her face. She didn't deserve that! No matter what he thought she'd done, she didn't deserve that. Why was he being so hateful? He must have known she had nothing to wear but this borrowed nightgown. It wasn't as if she'd arrived at this God-forsaken place with a trunkful of clothes and still chose to wander around the house in her nightgown. Besides, she hadn't known he was here when she came to the room. She'd only come to see Shelley.

She felt lightheaded and reached for the tall post at the foot of the bed as she lowered herself to the edge of the mattress. She didn't hear David move, but then he was there in front of her, hunkered down, his face on a level with hers, the icy skepticism melted from his eyes. "Robyn!" His voice was husky. "Damn, I forgot you'd been injured and traumatized in that crash, too. Are you all right?"

He gently brushed the hair back from the purple bruise and swore. "I should have given you something for the pain," he muttered. "I wasn't thinking straight. Apparently, I'm still not."

His hand cupped her cheek, and she moved her head against it. He had nice hands, soft but strong, and right now she needed the caress of another human being.

For a moment they didn't move or speak. His fingers traced the bruise, and tears welled up in Robyn's blue-black eyes and trickled slowly down her cheeks. David's other hand cradled her head, and his thumbs wiped away the teardrops, only to have them replaced by more. He leaned forward and kissed the corners of her eyes where the tears originated; then, as if realizing what he was doing, he muttered an oath and stood.

His voice was harsh again as he said, "Don't cry. I can't stand it when women cry. Look, let me help you back to your room, and then I'll give you a pain pill. It's a good thing I always keep a large stock of emergency medical supplies up here."

Robyn swiped at her tears with the back of her hand. "No, I'm sorry for being such a baby, but you're pretty much of a brute yourself," she said, and hoped her voice didn't betray the tremor his touch had aroused. "I feel all right, really. I slept soundly and am rested now. I meant what I said about staying with Shelley. If you're worried about my qualifications, my mother runs a nursery school, and I helped her with it during the summers when I was in college. I know more about caring for small children than a lot of mothers do. She'll probably sleep now until morning, and I promise to call you if she wakes up and asks for you."

He looked skeptical. "How do I know I can trust you?"

She shrugged. "You don't. You'll just have to believe that I'm telling the truth."

He stiffened and glared at her. "Oh, sure, take the word of an empty-headed little drunk who can't even control a car!"

His words slashed at her raw emotions, and she stood and started blindly from the room. "I'm sorry. I won't bother you anymore," she said just before she ran head-on into him.

His arms closed around her to balance them both, and then held her as she leaned shakily against him. She wanted to stay there in the warm protection of his embrace. She liked the feel of his breath on her cheek, of his hands moving up and down her spine like a caress, of his solid body pressed so firmly against hers that she could feel the flexing of his muscles.

His lips teased her ear lobe as he whispered, "You're trembling. Are you cold?"

She snuggled against him, and his arms tightened. What was the matter with her, anyway? This man was not only a stranger but one that had every intention of putting her in jail if he could. He hated her, and she knew that for her own protection she should avoid him, but right now she needed someone so badly. Someone to hold her, comfort her, protect her. She'd been through a horrifying experience. Her car had hit a child, and she herself had been injured and badly shaken, but she had no one to turn to.

Everyone in this house, David especially, thought she was a reckless drunk driver and was responsible for the accident. She'd never been through anything like this before and had always had someone—parents, relatives, friends—to cushion the bumps for her. Now she was alone, trapped in an unfamiliar place with a houseful of hostile strangers and a little girl who might be seriously injured because Robyn had stupidly picked up a hitchhiker. If this man was willing to comfort her, even for a moment, she was willing to accept that comfort.

She was brought out of her reverie by David's voice repeating his question. "Robyn, answer me. Are you cold?"

"No—yes—maybe a little," she stammered into his shoulder. "David, I wasn't drunk. I swear I wasn't. I've never been drunk in my life."

If only she could make him understand, make him believe her. But then there was the problem of the man who wasn't there. At least he wasn't there by the time David had gotten to her car. What had become of him? Was he still wandering around outside in the storm?

David suddenly released her and stepped back, his voice once again grim. "Whether you were or not, you seem to be sober now, and I'm in worse shape than I thought." He shook his head as though to deny the tenderness he'd shown her. "If you still want to sit with Shelley, I'll go lie down for a while. I have to be clearheaded enough tomorrow to figure out how to get help up here. I've got to get Shelley to a hospital."

The anxiety in his voice told Robyn clearer than words how desperately afraid he was for his daughter. It wasn't enough that the child had been injured, but the telephone lines were down, and the road was closed by a rock slide, so no one could get in or out. Things like that just didn't happen except in low-budget horror movies.

David left but returned a few minutes later with a man's wine velour robe that he wrapped around her. She tried to thank him, but he left again without listening.

Robyn stood at the open window, watching as the hesitant light of dawn blinked out the twinkling stars. It was a glorious view of rugged, snow-capped mountains in the background and stands of pine and aspen trees still emerging from their struggle with darkness. There wasn't a cloud in the sky, and the only sign of last night's storm was the glistening wetness of the ground and trees. The thin air smelled fresh and crisp, and the birds chirped a song to the newly born day.

She'd just gotten Shelley to sleep again after the child had awakened frightened and in pain. Robyn had given her the pain pill David had left for her and then bathed Shelley's face, hand, and right leg in warm soapy water. In their anxiety to treat her injuries, nobody had thought to clean her up, and she was grimy from her tumble in the muddy road. When they got her to the hospital, maybe one of the nurses would wash her hair. Meanwhile, Shelley was comfortable again and had gone back to sleep, no doubt with help from the narcotic in the medication.

A male voice from behind her startled Robyn, and she jumped. "Robyn, what are you doing in here? Where's David?"

She turned to see Graham Welles, his hair tousled from sleep and a blue robe over his lighter blue pajamas. "I woke up a couple of hours ago and offered

to sit with Shelley so her father could get some rest."
She smiled. "It took a little doing, but he finally agreed
and went off to bed."

A look of surprise flitted across Graham's face. "Will
wonders never cease," he muttered. "He growled like a
wounded bear when I offered to spell him at about one
o'clock. What kind of magic did you work on him?"

Robyn shrugged. "He was exhausted, and I guess he
realized he couldn't go on like that."

Graham looked at the little girl on the bed. "How is
she?"

"She's a bit restless," Robyn said, "but she's not
running a temperature, and she's rational."

Graham's glance returned to Robyn, and he grinned.
"Where did you get that robe? You look like a little girl
playing dress up in her daddy's clothes."

She looked down at herself and giggled. "The fit does
leave a little to be desired. Dr. Christopher brought it
to me before he left to go to bed."

Graham's eyes widened. "You mean you were running around in here in nothing but that topless nightgown you were wearing earlier?"

"It's not topless," Robyn snapped, even as her face
flushed red with embarrassment when she remembered
how revealing it was. "It's all I had to wear, and I didn't
know Dr. Christopher would be in here when I came
looking for Shelley."

Graham held up his hands in amusement. "Don't
apologize to me, beautiful. I only wish I'd been here.
No wonder poor old Dave bolted. I'm sure it's not
every night he's confronted by a gorgeous redhead
running around half naked and offering to do him
favors." He chuckled with mirth. "God, that must have
really rattled his nervous system!"

Robyn didn't find it funny and told him so. "Mr. Welles," she grated. "I was not offering him 'favors,' as you so crudely put it. I'd had plenty of sleep, and he hadn't, so I—"

"Hey, calm down." Graham laughed. "I was only teasing." He sobered and looked at her. "I'm sorry, Robyn. I know what a strain you're under. I was only trying to lighten it a little. I apologize for my clumsiness. Now, if you promise not to call me Mr. Welles anymore and call me Graham, I'll go make us some coffee."

Robyn felt her anger drain away. He seemed like an honorable man, and he was only trying to be nice. For that she was most thankful. She needed a friend.

She relaxed and said, "All right—Graham—I could use a cup of coffee."

"You got it," he said, and left.

He returned about ten minutes later with a tray bearing an insulated coffee server, cream, sugar, thick mugs and a plate heaped high with warm buttered toast. The mingled fragrances teased her nostrils, and it was only then that Robyn realized she was hungry. She hadn't eaten anything since lunch yesterday except for a few hors d'oeuvres at the cocktail party.

She poured the coffee and motioned Graham to sit in the upholstered chair while she settled herself cross-legged on the carpet in front of the floor-to-ceiling window. Graham sighed and lowered himself beside her, complaining all the while that he was much too old for sprawling around on the floor.

"I told you to take the chair," she said laughing.

He settled heavily and groaned. "It wouldn't have

been very gentlemanly of me to sit in the only chair while you huddled on the floor."

Robyn handed him a piece of toast. "I don't think you could ever be anything but a gentleman, Graham."

The hand holding the toast stopped halfway to his mouth, and his eyes searched her face. When he spoke, it was completely off the subject. "You're in bad trouble, Robyn, and don't count on David not pressing charges. He adores his daughter. She's all he's got now. If anything happens to her . . ."

His voice faded, and he took a swallow of his coffee, while Robyn looked away and cupped her suddenly cold hands around the warm mug. Would this nightmare never end? Surely she would awaken soon and find that it was all a ghastly dream.

She took a deep breath and said, "I wasn't driving that car, Graham. I know you don't believe me— nobody does—but there was a man, a man I didn't know, with me, and he's the one who lost control of the car and hit Shelley. I was knocked unconscious, and when I came around, he was gone."

"Don't tell me about it, Robyn," Graham warned. "Don't talk to me at all about the accident. I'm David's attorney. Take my advice and don't talk to anyone, not even the police, about this until you have consulted a lawyer of your own. I don't want you to incriminate yourself."

"I can't incriminate myself," she insisted. "I'm not guilty of anything but bad judgment in giving a ride to a stranger."

Graham reached over and patted her hand. "Eat your toast before Shelley wakes up and starts demanding attention."

Robyn took a bite of toast and a sip of coffee, then asked, "Graham, what was that child doing outside in the storm, anyway?"

Graham frowned. "I can't discuss it with you."

She was undeterred. "Where is Shelley's mother?"

"Belinda? That's a good question," he said. "Last I heard, she was in Hollywood making a movie."

"She's an actress?"

"That's a matter of opinion," Graham muttered. "She's beautiful, and has a throaty, sexy voice. I suppose that's all she really needs, especially in Hollywood. She gave up her daughter and put her husband through hell in the pursuit of her career. With that kind of ambition, she'll probably make it big whether she has any actual talent or not."

"She and Dr. Christopher are divorced?"

Graham nodded. "Yeah, David finally gave up trying to keep that farce of a marriage together and gave her her freedom. Poor bloke," he mused. "He was really crazy about her. Dave's the quiet type, never asked for much out of life, just a wife, a family and his career as a veterinarian. Instead, he got a father who was determined his only son would take over the family oil business—and Belinda."

Robyn was puzzled. "But he is a veterinarian, isn't he?"

"Sure is. And a damn good one, but he had a row with his father over it, and the old man never forgave him. Fortunately, he didn't cut David out of his will completely, but when he died, he left most of his stock to a favorite nephew. David got enough to live comfortably on, even if he hadn't had a lucrative practice, but the rift between him and his father nearly broke his heart. Then Belinda came along and finished the job."

Robyn felt a wave of compassion for the angry man who was determined to ruin her. He'd lost his father, the family business and his wife, and now his daughter was seriously injured, and there was no way to get help for her. No wonder he wasn't inclined to listen to Robyn's highly unlikely alibi.

She was pondering all this when a voice from the doorway made her jerk and spill her coffee. "How cozy."

David's glare was equally divided between Robyn and Graham, and his voice was tight and angry. "A picnic. I don't suppose it's occurred to either of you to check and make sure Shelley was all right."

He focused his attention on Robyn. "I should have known I couldn't trust you, not if there was a man around to seduce!"

Chapter Three

From her seat on the floor, Robyn stared up, wide-eyed with shocked disbelief, at the man towering over her. She opened her mouth, but the voice that sounded in the stillness was not hers but Graham's. "That remark was totally uncalled for, old chum."

There wasn't a shred of friendliness in his tone as he hoisted himself awkwardly off the floor and stood facing David. "As you can see, Shelley is sleeping comfortably, and Robyn and I were doing nothing more sinful than having coffee together. The fact that we were sitting on the floor was not, I assure you, from choice. If you'll bother to look around, you may notice that there is not an abundance of adult seating space in this nursery."

He turned away from a glowering David to help Robyn to her feet. She stood quaking before David, bewildered by his harsh accusation. What kind of man was he, anyway? How could he be so cold and domineering one moment and so warm and gentle the next?

Would she ever understand him? Did he even understand himself?

His glance raked over her, then turned to Graham. "You'd better be glad I got here first," he said mockingly. "As I passed your room, I heard Eve asking Irene if she'd seen you. If she'd found you and this little bit of fluff cavorting around on the floor in your night clothes, you wouldn't have stood a snowball's chance in Hades of getting her to listen to an explanation."

Graham blanched and swore. "Just what I need," he muttered as he ran his hand through his uncombed hair and started toward the door.

"As soon as I've had some breakfast, I'm going to try to climb over that rock slide in the road and hitchhike a ride to a telephone," David added. "If you can tear yourself away—" he looked pointedly from Graham to Robyn and back—"I'd appreciate some company."

"Of course," Graham answered stiffly. "I'll be ready any time you are." He strode quickly out of the room.

Without a word, Robyn gathered up the coffee things and left as well.

She reached her room just in time to meet Irene coming out of it with the blue jump suit over her arm. She greeted Robyn and said, "Your outfit is dry. I'm just going to press it. It won't take a minute."

Robyn stopped her. "There's no need to press it, Irene. That's one of the new crush-proof fabrics." She reached out to take the jump suit and hold it in front of her. "See, it looks just fine. Thanks so much for washing it for me."

She wasn't going to tell Irene that by laundering the garment she had disposed of vital evidence.

Irene nodded and disappeared down the stairs.

Inside the bedroom, Robyn was relieved to find that someone had retrieved her purse from the car and put it on the dresser. In the bathroom she found a clean glass, a toothbrush and a tube of toothpaste on the vanity. Apparently, Dr. Christopher took good care of his guests and any unwelcome strangers who wandered in, she mused.

After washing up and dressing, Robyn went in search of the others. She found them in the kitchen, a large cheerful room with avocado-green appliances and dotted Swiss ruffled curtains in a matching color at sun-filled windows. Still she felt a chill as soon as she stepped into the room. Graham and David were seated at the bright-yellow Formica-top table, talking to two women who could only be Eve Welles, Graham's wife, and her sister, Joyce Fredericks.

When Robyn appeared, the conversation ceased abruptly, and they all looked up at her. She was disconcerted by their silence and what could only be called their hostile stares. "I'm sorry. Am—am I interrupting?"

The woman Robyn assumed to be Eve looked at her coldly. A tall, skinny woman, all angles, she appeared to be in her early thirties. The type who looked underfed in person but whose photographs modeling expensive clothes were very *haute couture*. She wore her long black hair in a severe chignon on the top of her head, and her deep-chocolate designer jeans and color-coordinated top matched her eyes.

"As a matter of fact—" she started to say, but Graham interrupted.

"Of course not, Robyn," he said as he rose and held a chair for her.

Eve threw him a nasty look, but he ignored her and seated Robyn, then said, "Irene is giving Shelley her breakfast, so what can I get for you? How about scrambled eggs and bacon? They're all fixed here in the warming oven."

"Really Graham," Eve snapped. "I see no reason for you to be waiting on this—this woman. It's not as though she were a guest here. If she wants breakfast, she can serve herself."

Robyn cringed and felt the hot color of embarrassment sweep over her as she rose so quickly that she upset her chair. "Of course there's no need to wait on me. I—"

Surprisingly, David came to her rescue. He looked at Eve balefully as he rose and picked up the fallen chair. "That's enough, Eve," he said, and there was a warning in his voice.

He took Robyn's arm and seated her back in the chair without giving her a chance to protest. "Stay there," he commanded, then turned to face Graham, who was glaring at Eve. "You sit down, too, Graham, and I'll bring Robyn her breakfast."

Robyn was too mortified to do anything but sit still, looking down at the table and hoping the floor would open up and drop her from sight.

David brought her a plate of scrambled eggs, bacon and light, fluffy baking-powder biscuits. She couldn't look at him but murmured her thanks as he poured coffee in a mug and handed it to her.

The strained silence around the table was broken when David sat down again and spoke to Graham. "The telephone is still out of order, so we'll have to hike to the highway where hopefully we can thumb a ride into Nederland. I'm going to try to arrange for a helicopter to fly Shelley and me to a hospital. The forestry service will help."

He swallowed the last of his coffee and stood up again. "Can you be ready to go in fifteen minutes? Don't forget to wear boots." He left, and the others continued eating.

Robyn's appetite had disappeared, but she forced herself to eat until Graham left the kitchen; then she gave up all pretense as the two women turned to her. Eve again led off the conversation. "I guess if we're going to be thrown together most of the day, we'd better introduce ourselves. I'm Eve Welles, and this is my sister, Joyce Fredericks."

Robyn nodded in response and answered, "I'm Robyn Flannery, but I expect you know that by now."

"Yes, we do," Joyce muttered. It was the first time she'd spoken, and Robyn was surprised by her soft, southern accent. There had been no trace of it in her sister's voice.

Their speech pattern wasn't the only difference in the sisters. Joyce bore no physical resemblance to Eve. She was about Robyn's size, five feet four inches and slender, with chestnut hair and tawny eyes that were flecked with gold. Robyn guessed that Joyce was at least five years younger than her sister, but the two women had one thing in common—their utter contempt for Robyn.

Joyce continued speaking. "My, but that's a nasty bruise on the side of your face. And look"—she pointed so Eve wouldn't miss it—"she's got a black eye. You'll have to admit you got off darn easy, though, considering what you did to poor little Shelley."

Robyn knew it was going to be a long day.

She closed her eyes for a moment before she said, "I wasn't driving the car. There was a man with me, a man who seems to have disappeared."

Those words were beginning to sound like a litany, and Robyn knew it was an exercise in futility to keep repeating them. But she was not going to take the blame for hitting a child when she didn't do it.

Both women stared at her and said almost in unison, "You're kidding!"

Robyn clenched her fists in her lap and shook her head. She started at the beginning and told them the whole story, from her reasons for going to the cocktail party in Nederland to the blow that had knocked her unconscious as the car screeched to a halt on the slippery road.

The sisters looked at one another and then at Robyn. Eve spoke first. "That was a performance that would rival anything I've seen Belinda Christopher do. You know, you almost had me believing you until I remembered that you were strapped into the driver's seat with a seat belt and were slumped over the steering wheel when we got there."

Joyce nodded agreement as she sneered. "You'd better get your act together, lady, before you present it to David. He's been lied to often enough by Belinda, who's an expert, and he's sure not going to believe that crazy mixed-up story. If you take my advice, you won't even try it on him."

Robyn stood up and carefully pushed in her chair before she spoke. "I've told you the truth. I don't know how I got behind the steering wheel. I can only assume that the man took the time to slide me over there and fasten me in with the seat belt before he ran off. If he did, it was a smart move because now nobody's looking for him."

She turned and walked out of the kitchen.

After David and Graham left, Robyn went upstairs to Shelley's room, thinking she might be able to entertain the little girl for a while. Joyce was already there, though, reading aloud from a large illustrated volume of *Grimm's Fairy Tales*. Shelley seemed delighted to see Robyn, but Joyce dismissed her coldly. "Please don't bother Shelley, Robyn," she said, "Eve and I will see that she's *properly* taken care of."

Robyn decided that if she was not to be allowed near Shelley, she'd take a look at her car and see what damage had been done to it. She'd hardly touched the door handle when Eve came hurrying out with a cryptic message. "David left strict orders that you were not to touch that car," she announced scornfully. "There'll be no tampering with the evidence, so go on back to the house and stay away from the scene of the accident."

Robyn said nothing. She could only come out the loser in an argument with any of these people. It was useless to try to reason with them, and she'd had enough of their nastiness.

She followed Eve back to the house and went up to her room to lie down. She was more shaken up than she'd realized, and her hands trembled as she unbuckled her fragile high-heeled sandals and stretched out on the bed.

She was awakened later by a loud whirring sound outside and by excited voices and hurrying footsteps inside. She jumped off the bed and looked out the window in time to see a small helicopter setting down on the road in front of the house. David and Graham had finally gotten help!

Robyn quickly put on her sandals and hurried downstairs just as David and a tall young man dressed in coveralls came in the front door, guiding a low stretcher on wheels. They were followed by Eve, Joyce and Irene, who had apparently gone out to meet them. Graham came last, carrying a bag that Robyn assumed held emergency medical supplies.

Nobody paid any attention to her as they trooped past her and followed David and the stretcher up the stairs. Thank God they were going to take Shelley to a hospital!

Robyn knew they neither needed nor wanted her up there, and she paced around the lower level listening to the sounds from the top floor. Shelley's voice was protesting, David's reassuring, Joyce's coaxing and Irene's offering false cheer.

If everyone would just get out of there and let David handle Shelley, she wouldn't be so frightened, Robyn thought. She'd cared for sick and injured children in her mother's nursery school and knew that the more people fussed over them, the more insecure they felt.

Finally, after what seemed like hours, she heard them coming back down: the hum of the wheels on the stretcher, the clomp of various-sized and -weight shoes on the hallway, and the voices, all talking at once, trying to reassure the small girl and only frightening her more.

When they got to the front hall, Robyn saw that Shelley looked white and scared. She wanted to go to her, smooth the dirty, tousled hair from her forehead and plant a reassuring kiss on her nose, but again nobody paid her any attention as she huddled against the wall out of the way.

It wasn't until the procession stopped before going out the door to listen to last-minute instructions from David, who obviously was going with Shelley to the hospital, that the child caught sight of Robyn. Robyn quickly put her fingers to her lips and blew Shelley a kiss. For the first time, Shelley's little mouth lifted at the corners, and she blew a kiss back to Robyn.

Out of the corner of her eye, Robyn saw David watching the little exchange.

She followed them outside and stood on the porch watching as the entourage proceeded to the helicopter and the stretcher was lifted aboard. David then cut from the rest of the group and started back toward the house.

Robyn thought he was coming back to get something, but instead, he climbed the steps and stood in front of her. Their eyes caught and held, and she felt a warm weakness steal over her, felt the same magnetic pull that had left her powerless to resist during the night when he had held her face in his hands and kissed away her tears. She wanted to feel his hands on her again, his lips caressing her, his hard body—

Robyn jerked her thoughts back to reality and looked away, but she thought she heard a slight tremor in David's voice as he said, "I hope to be back tonight, but no matter how long I'm gone, you are to stay here until I return."

She blinked with surprise. "I can't very well go anywhere until they clear away the rock slide."

He nodded. "Just hold that thought. I'll see that you're examined by a physician as soon as we can get back to Boulder, but meanwhile, should you take it into your pretty head to run off, I won't hesitate to have you hunted down by the police."

He stomped back down the stairs and ran to the helicopter.

Robyn turned and wandered back into the house, feeling uncertain and depressed. There was no doubt that David intended to prosecute her. What on earth was she going to do? She would be fired from the chorus, her parents would be heartbroken, and where would she get the money for a lawyer to defend her?

Robyn heard the helicopter lift off and knew the other members of the household would be coming right in. She detoured into the small room where she had been brought after the accident last night and hoped no one would come looking for her. She had no desire to spar with them again during lunch.

The sound of voices reached her from the kitchen as she sank down on the sofa and glanced at her watch. One o'clock. It would be hours before David got back, if he came back. If Shelley was more seriously injured than they'd thought, then he wouldn't be back at all. Oh, God, if anything happened to that child—

A wave of despair washed over Robyn, and tears burned her eyes. Even though she knew she hadn't been driving the car when it had hit the little girl, she still felt responsible. If she hadn't made the colossal mistake of letting a strange man talk her into giving him a ride and then compounded it by letting him drive, none of this would have happened.

As far back as she could remember, her mother had admonished her not to accept rides with strange men. As she got older and started to drive, the no-no changed to "Don't pick up hitchhikers."

Only once had she forgotten her training, and that

was yesterday when she'd taken pity on a stranger and given him a ride.

Robyn got up and started to pace. But darn it, he hadn't really seemed like a stranger. She knew he'd been at the party—he was on the porch as she was leaving—and that meant he was involved in some way with the theater-in-the-round. A fellow cast or crew member was considered part of the theater family.

She stopped her pacing, struck by a thought so simple she was astounded that she hadn't thought of it before. He was a member of the cast or crew! That meant he would be at the tent either rehearsing with the cast or taking care of the technical end of the production. She could point him out to David, confront him, make him confess.

Robyn sank back down on the sofa, weak-kneed with relief. Of course he would probably deny her accusations, but once she knew who he was, she would find a way to prove he had been with her. He must have shown up somewhere soaking wet and badly shaken last night. Maybe he'd even been injured.

She discarded that thought as unlikely. He couldn't have put her in the driver's seat, fastened the seat belt and taken off so quickly if he'd had any disabling injuries. Still, there must be—

Her musings were interrupted by Graham, coming into the room with a tray in his hands. "So here you are," he greeted her. "You didn't show up for lunch, so I had Irene fix you a sandwich and a cup of coffee."

He set the tray on the desk and brought the plate and mug to her. Robyn smiled and said, "Thank you, Graham. That's very thoughtful of you."

He shrugged and sat down beside her on the couch. "Not really," he said. "I should have come and invited you to join us in the kitchen, insisted if necessary, but I figured you wanted to avoid another go-around with Eve and Joyce."

Robyn took a sip of coffee, using it as an excuse to not look at him or answer him.

After a moment, he continued. "I'm afraid I was as anxious to avoid a scene as you were. If Eve had gotten nasty with you, I'd have had to intervene, and Eve is difficult enough to live with without deliberately setting her off."

Robyn set down her coffee cup and spoke quickly before he could continue. She liked Graham, but she had no desire to listen to his marital problems, which were no doubt many and varied with a wife like Eve. "Please, don't apologize. I understand. I really can't blame any of you for feeling about me the way you do. If I'd done what you believe I did, I would be utterly reprehensible. But Graham, I've just thought of something. I think I can find the man who was with me. You see, I'd been to this cocktail party in Nederland and—"

"Robyn, stop right there," Graham broke in. "I told you, you mustn't discuss the events leading up to the accident with me or anyone else until you've consulted with an attorney. I'm David's lawyer, honey. I'm the enemy."

She sighed impatiently. "But I haven't done anything wrong! If you'd just listen to me—"

Graham shook his head and stood. "No, Robyn. Now eat your lunch and try to relax. As soon as we get back to Boulder, I'll find you a good defense attorney, and you can tell your story to him. While David and I were in Nederland this morning, we reported the telephone out of order and the rock slide across the road, and we were assured they'd have crews out today to see what could be done. Hopefully, we'll be able to go home tomorrow."

He turned to leave, then looked back at her. "And Robyn, for your own sake, don't make up any more stories."

She dropped her head in her hands and swore. It was no use. Even Graham didn't believe her. He was nice to her—he was apparently willing to forgive her—but he still believed that she was driving the car when it had struck Shelley.

It was midafternoon before the telephone rang and the repairman reported that it was once more operational. A short time after that, several men arrived in a jeep to assess the possibilities of clearing the road of the huge rocks. They assured Graham they'd have a crew out first thing the next morning to begin work.

Irene held dinner until eight o'clock waiting for David, but then announced it would be ruined if they didn't eat immediately. She had just started to serve the meal when David walked in the front door. Everyone jumped up from the table and ran to greet him. Inquiries about Shelley rang through the house as Robyn followed silently behind the rest.

She was the pariah here, the outcast, the untouchable. She saw David standing in the middle of the living room, surrounded by the others, who were firing questions at him. He looked tired, emotionally exhausted, but some of the tenseness was gone from his face, and he smiled as he said, "Shelley's had a thorough physical, and there's no sign of any other injuries. The doctors say I did a good job of setting her leg and suturing her elbow, and the X-rays and blood tests showed no further problems. They want to keep her at the hospital for a couple of days for observation, but it's just a precaution. She's going to be fine."

Robyn sagged against the wall as a wave of relief surged through her, leaving her trembling and unable to stand without the solid support. Shelley was going to be all right! She would suffer no permanent damage as a result of the accident!

Tears welled up past her throat, squeezed through her closed eyelids and rolled down her cheeks as she fought desperately to control them. She hated to cry, hadn't done so in years, but in the past few hours, she'd become a veritable waterworks.

She had to get out of there before someone saw her, but in her haste Robyn forgot that her knees were like Jell-O and her head was spinning. She took a few steps and stumbled, right into a pair of arms that caught and held her.

Even though she was blinded by tears, she knew it was David. The feel of his broad chest under her cheek, the tangy citrus aroma of his shaving lotion, mingled with the natural musky scent of him, and the hard, muscular thighs that pressed against hers were all impressions that would be branded into her nervous system for the rest of her life.

It wasn't a cheerful thought, and the cursed tears flowed freely as he cradled her to him and murmured, "Come now, you're going to be sick if you don't pull yourself together."

"Oh, really, David, she's just playing on your sympathy." Joyce's petulant voice cut through David's tenderness. "She's been just fine all day."

Robyn winced and tried to draw away, but David's arms tightened as he spoke. "I don't remember asking for your opinion, Joyce. Irene," he added, "take these people to the kitchen and start serving dinner. Robyn and I will be there in a few minutes."

There was a protest from Eve, but David paid no attention as he turned Robyn, and his arm still around her waist, led her into the library.

He seated her on the sofa, then went to the free-standing bar to mix himself a drink. "What will you have?" he asked.

"Nothing, thank you," Robyn answered, watching as he reached for another bottle and poured amber liquid into a brandy snifter.

He brought both drinks with him and handed her the snifter. "Here," he said as he seated himself beside her, "drink it. It will help you get control of yourself."

She wrinkled her nose. "I don't like brandy. I seldom drink anything." She sighed as she saw him frown. "I know you don't believe that, but it's true."

"Drink the brandy," he ordered, and Robyn knew it would do no good to argue.

The liquor was smooth and burned just a little as it slid down her throat. Almost immediately, a warm flush spread through her, and she felt calmer.

"Better?" David asked as she wrapped her hands around the sparkling crystal.

"Much," she murmured.

He took a swallow of his drink. "They've been giving you a bad time today, haven't they?"

She didn't have to ask who "they" were, but neither was she going to run to David with her problems. "Not really," she denied. "I—I was just so relieved to hear that your daughter isn't seriously hurt."

"Yes," he agreed. "So am I. I'd like to have stayed in Boulder tonight to be close to her, but I decided I'd better get back here and make sure they clear that road tomorrow."

Robyn set her nearly untouched drink on the table. "How did you get here? I didn't hear the helicopter."

David laughed. "No, the government doesn't run a taxi service with those things. That was only to get Shelley out of here and to the hospital. I had Will Otto, the gardener and handyman at my home in Boulder, drive me to the turnoff. I walked the rest of the way."

He took a long swallow of his drink and leaned back on the sofa. He closed his eyes and murmured, "I didn't realize until now how tired I am."

His face was gray with exhaustion, and without thinking, Robyn leaned over and traced the deep lines around his mouth with her finger. His skin was rough with a light stubble of beard, and she felt a muscle twitch as her finger moved gently over it.

David opened his eyes and looked at her, a question forming in the green depths. She quickly withdrew her hand, but he intercepted it and brought it back to his face. "Don't stop," he said, and closed his eyes again.

Her fingertips lightly massaged his cheek, then moved up to the tiny squint lines at the corner of his eye. He sighed softly, and she felt him relax under her touch.

She wished she could follow with her lips the path her fingers were taking. Would he like that? Most men would if the right woman was doing it, but she wasn't the right woman. He had Joyce for that sort of thing, and maybe once in a while, his ex-wife.

The sound of footsteps warned that someone was coming, and Robyn twisted around quickly and sat up just as Eve appeared in the doorway. Eve's dark eyes assessed the situation—David sprawled in a comfortable half-sitting, half-lying position against the back of the couch and Robyn looking flustered and slightly rumpled. Her voice was accusing as she said, "Look, David, I know it's none of my business but—"

David made no move to sit up, and his voice was drowsily content. "You're right, Eve, it is none of your business. Now, what can we do for you?"

Eve flushed angrily and snapped, "Please yourself, but if you don't come to dinner soon, your food is going to be cold." She turned and walked stiffly away.

The intimate mood between David and Robyn deteriorated rapidly from then on. The only two empty chairs at the table were at opposite ends, and Robyn was seated between Irene and Graham. David sat between Eve and Joyce, and the two sisters managed to monopolize the conversation.

For a while, Irene and Robyn discussed Irene's family, a son and daughter and three grandchildren, all of whom lived in other states, but when Irene rose to serve the dessert, Graham turned to Robyn and said, "Are you okay, Robyn? You really look beat. How's your head? That was a nasty bump you got."

Robyn smiled at him, grateful for his concern. "I'm fine, Graham, just a little—"

Eve's voice cut Robyn's sentence short. "It's no wonder she looks like hell. She's probably got a king-sized hangover. I hope you realize how lucky you are," she continued, "that Shelley's injuries weren't more serious. She could have been killed the way you were driving."

Robyn's stomach twisted painfully, as though she had been punched, and she hoped she wasn't going to be sick. When would she learn to keep her guard up around these people? They seemed to enjoy setting her up just to knock her down again. Well, she wasn't going to let them intimidate her.

She took a deep breath and said, "It is indeed fortunate that Shelley escaped more serious damage, and I am delighted that she will be out of the hospital soon. But I was not drunk last night, and I was not driving that car. If you would only believe me and look for the man—"

She paused as David's icy gaze fastened on her. Those jade eyes that had looked at her so warmly less than an hour ago now blazed with a cold anger, and his voice echoed his rage. "You can stop lying now, Robyn. It's too late to do a blood test on you, and the rain washed away the skid marks. Since Shelley's negligence contributed to the accident, I don't imagine you will be convicted of anything, so please spare us your preposterous stories."

Robyn felt a matching rage rising in her. Damn him, he didn't even try to understand. He had his narrow little mind made up, and he wasn't about to have it changed. Well, there was one thing she was going to get settled right now.

She met his ice with fire as she grated, "You're right. Shelley did contribute to the accident by running right in front of the car. And where were you? Why did you allow her out in that violent storm, alone and unattended? Who are you to sit there pompously blaming me when you can't even keep track of your own child?"

Her words hung in the silence of the room as the blood drained from David's already pale face and the ice in his eyes turned to anguish. His shoulders slumped, and he dropped his head in his hands for a moment, then raised it and looked at her. "You're right, of course. I must share the blame for what happened to my daughter." His voice had a tight, strangled quality. "I should have been watching her more closely. She'd taken Jenny Lind, her canary, out of the cage when the dog, who had been outside, started scratching to get in. She opened the door for the dog, and the canary flew out of the house. Her only thought right then was to get the bird back, and she ran out into the storm. She was trying to follow Jenny Lind's flight and didn't pause to look as she ran into the road."

His gaze continued its relentless hold on Robyn. "I'm responsible for her being in the road, and you're to blame for hitting her."

Robyn would have sold her soul to take back her accusations. She'd had no idea that David was blaming himself as well as her for the accident. If she had known, she'd never have taunted him so cruelly. She wanted to tell him how sorry she was, to reach out to him, to erase the agony that looked out of his eyes.

Instead, all that came out was "I didn't know you had a dog."

He pushed his chair back and stood, still looking at her. "The dog apparently ran off and hasn't been seen since. I suspect he's beneath the rock slide."

He walked out the kitchen door and let it slam behind him.

Robyn woke from a sound sleep to darkness and the feeling that something alarming had awakened her. She rolled over and tried to focus her eyes in the dark, but the drapes were pulled across the windows, and she could see nothing.

Then it came again. A noise, the sound of muted footsteps right there in the room. She raised herself up on her elbow and called, "Who's there?" in an unsteady voice.

"Don't be frightened, Robyn. It's only me." It was David's voice, and as he spoke, he switched on the lamp between the two beds.

Robyn clutched the sheet to her as she sat up, her eyes wide with surprise. David was standing between the beds wearing nothing but a pair of deep-wine pajama trousers. "What are you doing in my room?" she demanded.

His bare chest was broad and muscular and covered with a mat of blond hair, slightly darker than the hair on his head. His face was expressionless, and he replied, "You've got it all wrong. This is my room. You're the intruder."

"But you put me here," she gasped. "Or at least you told Irene to."

He turned back the covers on the other bed. "That's right, I did. It's the only extra bed in the house. What are you complaining about? The mattress is soft, and the sheets are clean."

Robyn threw her legs over the side of her bed and started to get up. "Oh, no," she grated. "I'm not playing your nasty little game. I'll sleep on the couch."

Before she could stand up, his voice, harsh and cold, stopped her. "Lie back down, Robyn. I'm not going to let you create a scene and disturb the whole household. I'll sleep on the couch, but even if I insisted on occupying the second bed in here, you'd be safe with me. I'm not interested in you, and if I were, I'm too tired to do anything about it."

He picked up his pajama top and slipped it on, his fingers working at the buttons as he headed for the door.

Robyn's curiosity got the better of her, and she called after him. "Dr. Christopher?"

He turned, and his gaze lingered on her bare shoulders and arms. "You called me David when I held you in my arms this morning. Don't you think if you're going to sleep in my bed, you should call me by my first name?"

Robyn ignored the blush she could feel warming her face as she said, "I just wondered why you have two double beds in your room."

He grunted. "That's the way my wife wanted it. She preferred to sleep alone."

"I'm sorry," Robyn said, then realized it sounded ridiculous.

"No sorrier than I was. Now go back to sleep."

He walked out and shut the door quietly behind him.

Chapter Four

Robyn slept soundly and was wakened in midmorning by the racket of heavy earth-moving equipment. The road crews had apparently come to clear the rocks from the access road.

It was a beautiful day. The sun was shining, and the fresh, clean fragrance of pine reminded Robyn that she was in the middle of a forest. When she'd dressed and gone downstairs, Irene told her that David and Graham had gone to check the road-clearing operation and Eve and Joyce had just returned from driving them there.

They were sitting at the kitchen table talking when Robyn walked in. "I hope they get that mess cleared away today," Eve said as she lit one of her never-ending cigarettes. "I'm bored out of my skull sitting around here. Besides, I'm doing a fashion show tomorrow night, and I can't possibly miss it. Oh, Robyn." She turned as Robyn approached, and the discontented whine of her voice became more noticeable. "You're a real lady of leisure, aren't you? Do you always sleep this late?"

Robyn ignored the verbal thrust and poured herself a cup of coffee. "Sorry if I inconvenienced anybody," she said. "Have they any idea how long it will take to open the road?"

Joyce spoke up. "They call it a rock slide, but those aren't rocks. They're boulders. I don't know how they're ever going to move them. Tomorrow's Monday, and if I don't show up for work after already having a week off, my boss will be most unhappy."

She shuddered, and Robyn asked, "Where do you work?"

"I'm a secretary at the university," Joyce answered.

Robyn smiled. "I love that campus. I studied there for four years before I graduated a year ago."

Joyce grimaced. "Oh, you and Eve. You're both intellectuals. I took a quickie course at a business school in Memphis after I graduated from high school, and I've never been without a job."

"So you're from Tennessee," Robyn said. "How does it happen that you speak with a southern accent and Eve doesn't?"

"It didn't just happen," Eve broke in. "I worked hard to get rid of mine. When I first went to New York, I was doing television commercials, and the regional accent was a real drawback. Then, in a moment of weakness, I married Graham and let him talk me into settling out here where it doesn't matter how I talk."

Robyn didn't care for the casual way Eve dismissed her marriage as a weakness. "Don't you do television commercials anymore?" she asked as she sat down at the table.

"Once in a while in Denver," Eve answered, "but it's not big time like it was in New York. Here I'm mostly limited to working with photographers or in fashion shows."

She tapped the ashes off her cigarette and took a swallow of coffee, then looked at her sister. "Take my advice, Joyce, and forget your grand plans to marry a rich man and let him support you. Marriage is too limiting. You lose too much of your freedom."

They both seemed to have forgotten Robyn as Joyce shot back, "I'm not career-minded like you are. I want to be a rich man's wife with plenty of prestige and leisure time. It's a whole lot better than having to grub for a living on my own or marrying a laborer and having to support him, too."

Robyn sat quietly and drank her coffee. So that's what Joyce was after. She intended to marry David because he was rich and a member of the elite. It didn't matter whether or not she was in love with him!

Robyn shivered. David was too nice a man for a woman like Joyce. Surely he was intelligent enough not to let himself get trapped in a marriage like that. Still, he'd apparently married a woman who was totally wrong for him the first time. Maybe he'd turn right around and make the same mistake again.

The two men returned at lunch time to report slow going with the clearing operations. Eve and Joyce protested that they had to be back in Boulder by early the next morning. Robyn had the same sense of urgency but said nothing. She was due to start rehearsals Monday morning at eight, and Tyler Kerr, the temperamental young director, would not be understanding if she didn't show up. Still, there was nothing David could do about it, and she was hardly in a position to fuss at him.

David was polite but distant during lunch, which was served on the redwood deck off the kitchen. It was almost like picnicking in the forest, and Robyn was too enchanted with the sights and sounds and scents that surrounded her to feel left out as the others chatted about things she knew nothing of. She did ask David if he'd talked to the hospital. He said he'd phoned as soon as he got up and had been told that Shelley had slept peacefully all night and was still sleeping.

When they finished eating and the group had dispersed, Robyn stayed to drink another cup of coffee as she watched the squirrels scamper up and down the tall trees or sit upright on their haunches, feeding themselves with their handlike claws.

She breathed in the fresh, clear air, then jumped as a man's voice behind her said, "What are you doing out here alone?"

It was David, and Robyn looked around as he joined her at the railing. Without waiting for an answer, he posed another question, this time in a more intimate tone. "Did you sleep comfortably in my bed last night?"

She knew he was teasing and was glad he wasn't angry with her. She nodded. "Yes, I slept so soundly that I didn't wake up until all that heavy machinery started lugging boulders around. I—David, I'm sorry you had to sleep on the couch. That is, if that's where you slept."

Her face reddened as she realized that hadn't come out right. Darn, why hadn't she stayed off that subject?

David's glance was impatient. "And where else would I sleep if not on the couch?"

His hand moved toward her face, and she instinctively moved back as his fingers touched her forehead. "Stand still," he demanded. "I want to examine that bruise."

He brushed her heavy auburn hair back and probed the wounded area gently. His touch sent delicious little shivers through her, and she stiffened with the effort it took not to tremble. He misunderstood and muttered, "Relax. I'm not going to hurt you. The bruise is fading nicely, and the swelling is all gone around your eye. I'm sure your doctor will tell you you'll be as good as new in a few days."

She hoped so. The first musical of the season opened in just a week, and she didn't relish going on stage with a black eye even though it could be covered with pancake makeup.

Robyn turned back to the railing and sighed. "You're lucky to have a place like this where you can come to get away from all the pressures of city life. My parents could never afford much in the way of vacations." She smiled as her thoughts flitted backward. "One year they rented a cabin in the woods for a week. It was nothing like this, just three rooms and a bath. My little sister and I slept on the pull-out couch, and my two brothers bunked on the floor in sleeping bags. Still, it was an exciting experience, a memory I've always cherished even though I did spend the whole week chasing those bratty little siblings of mine through the trees in an effort to keep track of them."

David grinned. "A regular little mother hen. Were there just four children in your family?"

"Yes, but Laurie and the boys are a lot younger than me, so I did a lot of baby-sitting. Laurie's only a year older than your Shelley."

"No wonder you were so good with Shelley," he murmured, then changed the subject. "Would you like to go for a walk in the woods?"

Robyn nodded enthusiastically. "Oh, yes," she said as she put her hand through the arm he offered and walked with him down the steps.

The terrain was rough, the path narrow, and it was difficult for Robyn to walk in her high-heeled sandals, but David walked slowly, and she managed to stay by his side. They wandered through juniper and pine, and occasionally a rabbit scampered across their path. Once, Robyn spotted a fawn standing in a meadow of wildflowers. They stopped and watched it for a few minutes until it raised its head, and apparently catching their scent, turned and bounded off in the opposite direction.

Robyn was enchanted, and David hugged her arm against him, explaining that it was a rather rare occurrence to see deer in the middle of the day, although they were a familiar sight in the mornings and evenings.

The path led upward, and after about thirty minutes, Robyn began to get winded, and her high heels were making her feet ache. When they came to a clearing, she suggested they rest for a while. David lifted her onto a fallen log, then hoisted himself up and perched beside her. From where they sat, they could see the towering, snow-covered, rocky crags in the distance where white clouds drifted above them.

Robyn took off her sandals and set them aside, tucking her stockinged feet beneath her. "If I owned a home up here, I'd never want to leave it."

David sat with his knees drawn up and his arms wrapped around his legs. "I'd like to spend more time here, but I do have a practice in Boulder that I can't neglect."

She sighed. "Of course. Do you close your office when you are gone?"

"Oh, no. I have two partners, and we operate an animal hospital. When one of us takes off, the other two fill in for him, but we're pretty busy, and the extra work means longer hours and more strain."

Robyn had an urge to know more about this handsome man who was doing strange things to her pulse and breathing. "Where did you get your training?"

"At U.C. Davis, in California," he answered. "It has one of the best schools of veterinary medicine in the world."

"Have you always wanted to be a veterinarian?" she continued. "Graham says your family was in the oil business."

David's mouth tightened into a thin line. "For an attorney, Graham has an awfully big mouth."

Robyn's eyes widened as she turned to look at him, realizing she'd gone too far. "Oh, David, I'm sorry. I didn't mean to pry. Graham didn't say anything much, really."

David relaxed a little and shook his head. "It doesn't matter. It's no secret that dad was mad as hell when I decided to be a vet instead of an oil baron. He never did forgive me."

He turned away, but Robyn had heard the tinge of regret in his tone. She impulsively put her hand on his arm and murmured, "I didn't mean to upset you."

He looked down at her and covered her hand with his. "You're a sweet child, Robyn. I'm surprised some man hasn't made you his own long before this."

She didn't like his patronizing attitude, and she slipped her hand from beneath his as she said, "I'm not a child. I'm twenty-three."

He laughed. "Have it your way, Ms. Flannery, but I'm thirty-five, and it seems a lifetime ago that I was your age." He looked at his watch and jumped down from the log. "I'm sorry to cut this short, but I've got to get back to the house and call the hospital. I want to talk to Shelley. I don't want her to think I've abandoned her."

He picked up her sandals. "Put out your feet and I'll help you back into these."

There was something awfully intimate about having David put her shoes on her. His hands cupped her feet almost caressingly, and he swore softly as his big fingers fumbled with the tiny buckles. When he'd finished with them, he put his hands at her waist and lifted her down. Robyn grabbed his shoulders for balance, and when he stood her on her feet, his grip on her tightened. His breath was warm on her cheek as he held her for a few seconds before he let her go. She took her hands from his shoulders quickly before she could hold on and refuse to be released.

As they started back, Robyn glimpsed a large animal running parallel to them through the trees. It was gone before David saw it, but he told her it was probably a deer or an elk.

"Do large animals like that live in this forest?"

"You bet," he assured her. "Also black bears and bighorn sheep, so don't go wandering around unless I'm with you."

She shuddered. "I won't. I promise. Do you treat big animals, David?"

He chuckled. "Not usually. We limit our practice to

house pets, although that sometimes includes exotic species like lynx, leopard and a wolf now and then."

His mood turned serious as he continued. "Actually, it's because of one of those big animals that I had the medical instruments I needed to set Shelley's leg and suture her arm. A couple of years ago, I found a magnificent buck that had been injured. He had a broken leg among other things, but I could have saved him if I'd had the proper equipment. Unfortunately, I didn't, and by the time I'd notified the forestry service and they sent somebody, it was too late."

He took a deep breath as though remembering even now was painful. "Since then, I've kept supplies up here to take care of such emergencies."

Robyn turned her head to look at him. He really was a caring person. How could his wife have preferred a career that presumably took her away for long periods of time to this tall, handsome and gentle man who, from all reports, had loved her dearly? Robyn had never had the burning urge to marry and start a family, but she'd never before met a man like David.

Last night, before sleep overtook her, she'd had vague, restless stirrings that she'd dismissed as lingering overtones of shock from the accident. Now she realized her unsettled state had been due to disappointment because David had not insisted on sharing the room with her.

Good heavens, he was a stranger! What was wrong with her, anyway? Was she really so desperate for a man?

She knew the answer to that. It wasn't just any man she wanted to share her bedroom with. It was this particular one. The man who thought she had hit his young daughter with her car!

Robyn became so entangled in her thoughts that she forgot to pay attention to where she was walking, and one of her high heels landed in a hole, throwing her off stride. She stumbled forward, but before she could fall, David caught her and balanced her against his full length.

The shock of his hard, muscular body pressed against her soft and yielding one replaced the trauma of the near fall. Robyn raised her head to find his face only inches from hers, his green eyes seeking her blue ones just before his mouth lowered to hers in a kiss of such tenderness that she couldn't have resisted if she'd wanted to. Her arms circled his lean waist, and she could feel the warmth radiating from his bare flesh beneath his T-shirt as she responded without reserve.

David lifted his head and smiled before his lips once more covered hers, but though the gentleness was still there, a new dimension had been added, a hunger he made no attempt to disguise. His arms pulled her even closer, and her hand found its way under his shirt to the smooth skin that covered the column of muscles on either side of his spine. Robyn felt the tremor that rippled through him at her touch, and his tongue teased her lips until they parted, allowing him to deepen the kiss.

His need had awakened an answering hunger in her, and she clung to him, forgetful of everything but his mouth on hers, his heart beating in the same erratic pattern as her own, and his hips and thighs pressed intimately against hers.

He seemed in no hurry to end the kiss, and when he did, he did it slowly, as though an abrupt separation would be too painful. Robyn's indigo eyes widened with disbelief as she whispered, "You said you weren't interested in me."

His smooth, freshly shaven cheek rubbed hers. "I lied," he said simply.

They returned to the house silently, hand in hand, and Robyn knew that an important change had taken place in her. She'd always been popular with the boys, and she'd been kissed and cuddled many times, but never before had it affected her so deeply. Her heart was beating wildly, and she felt both feverish and ecstatic.

There was no doubt that Dr. David Christopher was becoming too important to her, and she knew it was a dangerous situation. They'd known each other less than forty-eight hours, and they couldn't have gotten off to a worse start. David had no respect for her at all, and she was overly impressed with him. No relationship could exist on that basis, but if she didn't get away from there soon, she might do something really foolish, like letting him make love to her.

Just the thought of lying with him in an intimate embrace nearly undid Robyn, and she was appalled at her reaction. What was the matter with her, anyway? She was no love-starved teenager; she was a grown woman who had always had it all together. How could she be so stupid as to lust after a man who was not only rumored to be still in love with his ex-wife but who had a girl friend who was apparently more than willing to take care of his physical needs?

As they approached the clearing that surrounded the house, David stopped behind a flowering bush and cupped her face in his hands. All of the scolding she'd given herself evaporated as his lips touched hers briefly.

His voice was husky as he murmured, "This could become addicting," and took her mouth with a gentle sweetness that could easily drive her quite mad.

This time he broke it off abruptly and almost dragged her into the house.

They were greeted by the rest of the household; they demanded to know where they'd been for so long, and Robyn was surprised to learn that they'd been gone over two hours. David made some teasing remark about the big bad wolf waylaying Little Red Riding Hood in the forest, and all but Joyce laughed. She obviously failed to appreciate his humor.

After a few minutes, David excused himself to call the hospital in Denver. Somehow he maneuvered to casually take Robyn's arm and usher her up the stairs without the others noticing. He led her into his bedroom, which was hers temporarily, where there was a telephone and more privacy.

He sat down on one of the beds and motioned her to sit beside him as he dialed the number. "I thought you might like to talk to Shelley, too," he explained, and Robyn nodded.

David talked to his daughter for several minutes, then asked if she'd like to talk to Robyn. Apparently, Shelley agreed because he handed the phone to Robyn, then walked over to look out the window.

Robyn said cheerfully, "Hi, Shelley. How are you feeling?"

"I'm okay." The child sounded somewhat subdued.

Sympathy for the lonely little girl welled up in Robyn, and she tried to sound encouraging as she said, "Are they taking good care of you there at the hospital?"

"I guess so, but I hate it here. There's nothing to

do," Shelley wailed in the age-old complaint of a bored child.

"I'm sorry, honey," Robyn murmured. "If I were there, I'd play games with you. Do you like puzzles?"

"Oh, yes." Shelley's voice brightened. "And Monopoly and Clue and Chinese checkers. Will you come and see me as soon as you get home, Robyn?"

Robyn didn't know whether David would agree to that or not. He probably wouldn't want to have anything more to do with her when they finally got back to Boulder, but she couldn't say that to Shelley. She said instead, "Sure I will, but you probably won't be in the hospital much longer."

"I hope not." There was a pause, then Shelley said, "Robyn . . . umm . . . will you sing me a song?"

Robyn was a little startled by the request. "Now?"

"Uh huh. I like to hear you sing."

Robyn laughed softly. "Thank you, honey. Is there something you'd especially like to hear?"

Shelley thought for a moment, then said, "Do you know the Do, Re, Me song?"

"Sure," answered Robyn.

The delightful song was one of Robyn's favorites, and she hummed a few bars to find the right pitch before her rich alto voice filled the room with the lilting melody. She was conscious that David had turned and was watching her, and she added a few hand and facial gestures for his benefit.

David grinned, and Shelley insisted on an encore, which Robyn gladly performed. This time it was a catchy tune from one of the Disney movies, and David joined her on the chorus in a surprisingly good baritone. Shelley laughed and clapped and insisted on more. They entertained her for a few minutes longer before David reminded his daughter that they were talking long distance and it was time to call a halt.

He said good-by to Shelley and assured her he'd see her that night or tomorrow at the latest, then hung up.

He turned to Robyn, his expression happy and relaxed. "You have a beautiful voice," he said. "It's obviously trained."

She was delighted with his compliment and smiled. "Thank you, David. I majored in music with a minor in drama in college, and I make my living singing and dancing. I've traveled for the past year with a national company of *Annie,* and tomorrow I'm supposed to start rehearsals for the theater-in-the-round operettas that are being performed in Boulder this summer."

She'd been feeling so lighthearted and happy that she'd failed to notice the change in David's expression until she felt him stiffen. They had been standing close together as they shared the telephone mouthpiece while they were singing to Shelley, but now, although her arm still brushed his, they might have been miles apart, so complete was his withdrawal. The color had drained from his face, and he glared, not *at* her but *through* her.

Robyn was totally bewildered, and her voice wavered as she asked, "David, what's the matter? Did I say something wrong?"

This time his eyes focused squarely on her as he clenched his fists at his sides. "So you're an actress!" he snarled. "You had me almost believing— My God, I should have known!"

He turned and stalked out of the room.

Robyn lowered herself slowly to the side of the bed. What on earth had brought that on? She'd made no secret of the fact that she was a performer, but David acted as though he hadn't known.

She thought back. Maybe he hadn't. She remembered telling Eve and Joyce in detail about her profession when she'd tried to explain to them that she was not responsible for the accident that injured Shelley. And she'd answered the questions put to her by Graham in David's presence that first night, but had he actually asked her what she did for a living? Her mind had been so muddled that night, and she couldn't remember clearly.

Why would the fact that she was a singer and dancer matter to him, anyway? He'd called her an actress, but she'd never thought of herself as such. She was a performer, a member of the chorus with no lines to speak or solos to sing. She'd majored in music in college, not drama, and the only reason she'd tried out for the cast of the road show last year was because she and a classmate had been in New York at the time and the classmate had seen the ad and decided they should both have a go at it. Unfortunately, the classmate had been rejected, and Robyn hadn't heard from her since.

She got up and moved slowly about the room. Did the fact that his ex-wife was an actress have anything to do with David's outburst? According to Graham, she had put her career above everything, including her husband and daughter, but David had no right to assume Robyn was like Belinda. And even if she was, what difference did it make to him? He had shown her that he desired her physically, but most men didn't ask for a résumé before taking a pretty girl to bed.

Robyn stopped in front of the dresser and looked at herself in the mirror. Was it possible that he'd had something more permanent in mind? She leaned forward and examined the bruise that covered most of one side of her face. It wasn't likely that he'd been carried away by her beauty. Although the purple marks were fading, she still looked awfully battered.

No, David Christopher had no deep feelings for her. For one thing, there hadn't been time, and for another, he thought she was a reckless drunken driver and a liar. Still, this afternoon he'd been kind and thoughtful, and although he'd left no doubt about his desire for her, his kisses had been gentle, tender, even loving.

She drew away from the mirror and headed toward the door. It didn't matter why David was upset by the revelation that she was in show business. The fact that he was upset was enough reason for her to set the matter right. She'd tell him that she had no desire to be an actress, performer, whatever, that her career goal was to teach. She'd also tell him that she wanted a husband, a family and a home where she could put down roots. The last thing she wanted to do with her life was travel around the country with a theater group performing a night here, a week there, never having a person or a place to call her own.

The downstairs rooms were deserted with the exception of the kitchen. Robyn could hear Irene puttering around in there, but she was humming to herself in an absent-minded way that indicated she was alone. Robyn wandered through the empty rooms, then pushed open the front screen door and walked out onto the porch. Graham was sitting there on one of the heavily padded redwood lounge chairs.

He looked up and smiled. "Hi there, come sit with me. Would you like a beer?" He indicated the bottle he was holding.

"No, thank you," Robyn said. "I was looking for David. Have you seen him?"

"Just barely." He sounded amused. "He shot out the door like a bat out of Hades a few minutes ago and headed off down the road. I hollered at him, but I don't think he even heard me. Reminded me of the 'good old days' when he and Belinda used to have at it and he'd stalk off in a temper. Maybe he had a go-round with Joyce. She's been in a foul mood all afternoon."

Robyn shook her head and sighed. "No, I'm afraid it's me he's upset with, and I'm not even sure why. We'd been singing to Shelley on the phone, and afterward I mentioned that I sing and dance for a living, that I'm a member of the chorus at the theater-in-the-round this summer. He—he made some sarcastic remarks and stormed out of the room. He acted as though I'd just confessed to being a cut-rate call girl."

Graham looked at her for a long moment, then motioned to the lounge chair beside him. "Sit down, Robyn. There's no point in trying to catch up with him. Give him a chance to cool off a little and maybe then he'll be more reasonable."

Robyn settled down on the lounge, and Graham continued. "So you're in show business? What rotten luck. He would have been more understanding if you *had* confessed to being a lady of the night. That he could forgive, but anyone in show business is automatically scratched from his list of acquaintances. He'll be all the more determined to make you pay for what you did to Shelley now that he knows you're an actress."

"But I'm not an actress," Robyn protested. "And besides, that's unfair."

"Of course it is, honey," Graham sympathized, "but after what Belinda put him through, he's not about to get involved with another one of her ilk. He came out of that relationship hurting badly, and I really can't blame him for wanting to protect himself from more of the same."

Robyn opened her mouth to protest further just as Eve called to Graham from the house. Before he could answer, the screen door opened, and the woman herself appeared. "Graham—oh, there you are. I—" She broke off as she saw Robyn lounging in the chair next to Graham's.

Her voice changed to a strident tone. "For heaven's sake, Graham, can't you get off your lazy bottom and help me pack?"

Graham set down his beer bottle and answered, "I'm sorry, Eve. I didn't realize you were packing already. They haven't cleared the road yet."

"Well, they'd better have it opened by this evening," she stormed. "We all have to be back at work tomorrow morning, including you, and I want to be ready to leave as soon as the last boulder is hauled off. Now if you can tear yourself away from our charming little drunken driver here, I'd appreciate some help."

Graham swung his long legs over the side of the lounge chair and stood. His voice was harsh as he said, "There's no need to be nasty, Eve. I'm coming."

He flashed Robyn an apologetic smile and followed his wife into the house.

David didn't return until dinner time. Robyn was in the kitchen helping Irene with last-minute preparations when she heard footsteps on the porch and the screen door open and shut. She could see into the small entryway from where she stood at the table, and she looked up as David came into view. Before he could move on, Joyce came out of the living room where she, Graham and Eve were having cocktails.

David smiled at her and held out his arms. "Hi, beautiful. Come here. I've hardly seen you at all today."

Joyce snuggled into his embrace and lifted her face for a kiss that he was not at all reluctant to give. They seemed to melt together in the shadows, and Robyn gasped at the sudden pain that tore through her. David was kissing Joyce with just as much passion as he had kissed her earlier in the afternoon!

She watched, unable to tear her gaze away, as the pain mounted. It seemed like an eternity before the two lovers came up for air. When they did, Joyce whined petulantly, "It's not my fault you haven't seen me. You've been gone most of the day."

David's hands caressed her back through the clinging blouse she wore as he murmured softly, "Well, I'm here now, and I don't intend to let you out of my sight again tonight."

Chapter Five

Dinner was an unrelenting agony for Robyn.

David had returned with the news that the road wouldn't be open until sometime the next day. After a curt nod of greeting to Robyn, he studiously ignored her and lavished all of his considerable charm on Joyce, who lapped it up as a kitten does cream.

They sat close together, held hands and giggled as they murmured softly to each other. Irene's succulent meat loaf, tender baked potato with sour cream and chives and fresh green beans might as well have been sawdust. Robyn ate but tasted nothing. When dessert was served, she had an urge to grind her chocolate cream pie into David's smirking face.

How could he behave this way? She had been so sure that he was kind, considerate, a true gentleman, but now he was behaving like a lovesick fool, and she knew he wasn't. Up to now, his public attentions to Joyce had been friendly but not passionate. Now he was behaving as though he couldn't wait to haul her off to bed.

Well, if that was all he wanted, fine. Robyn was glad

she'd found out before she'd totally succumbed to his persuasive attempts at seduction. If he was that kind of man, she didn't want anything to do with him.

But how could she have been so totally wrong about him? She'd known dozens of seductive men, and they all had one thing in common, a dedicated self-centeredness. They were willing to lavish attention and gifts on a woman, but it was all directed toward achieving their own gratification. They would please women only if the women accommodated their needs.

Any pretty woman who wanted more from a man than a quick toss between the sheets in return for a gourmet dinner and a flashy piece of jewelry could spot that type before he even spoke. Robyn had become an expert at sighting and defusing them without causing a scene, so why had she been taken in by David? She sat in mute misery until the intolerable meal was over.

David and Joyce strolled off toward the woods, and Robyn felt sick. She wasn't about to let anyone else know what a gullible idiot she'd been, so she joined Graham and Eve in the parlor for after-dinner drinks. She settled for coffee and wondered if these people always drank so much—before dinner, with dinner, after dinner. If so, where did David get off rising up in righteous wrath over her practically nonexistent imbibing? But then he thought she had been driving the car while drunk and had hit his daughter.

It always came back to the accident. David would never believe the truth, would never forgive her for what he thought had happened. Add to that the fact that she was in show business and her degradation in his eyes was complete! She couldn't really blame him, but neither could she stay around and risk falling in love with him.

She heard David and Joyce returning sooner than she'd expected and hurriedly excused herself and went upstairs to her room before she had to face them again. She showered and washed her hair, then once again rinsed out her jump suit, underwear and pantyhose, the only clothes she had. She couldn't wait to get home and change into another outfit and made a vow to donate the silky jump suit to the first charity drive that came along. She hated the sight of it!

Robyn put on the nightgown Joyce had reluctantly loaned her and David's too-large robe and went back downstairs. She was careful to avoid attracting attention as she made her way to the small library. The room was seldom used, and she figured she could remain safely hidden there, away from Eve's carping and David's and Joyce's preliminary lovemaking.

She shivered with dismay and opened the book she'd been reading earlier. It was a weighty tome set back in the eleventh century, and it was evident that the author's interests were in authentic research rather than plot. She supposed it was the type of thing a man would enjoy, but she was soon nodding over it and having trouble keeping her eyes open.

She finally put the book down and turned out the light. She removed David's robe and stretched out on the couch, then pulled the robe over her and curled up under it. David could have his big room with the private bath back. He'd need it since he'd made no secret of the fact that he planned to entertain Joyce in his bed tonight. The couch was comfortable, and all Robyn wanted was to shut everything out of her mind and sleep.

Robyn was rudely awakened when the lamp just above her head was turned on. She shaded her eyes with her hand and saw David standing over her. He had an odd look on his face, and his voice was gruff but with a slight quiver as he spoke. "What are you doing in here? You damn near scared the hell out of me! I had visions of you wandering alone and unprotected through the forest—"

Now she recognized the look. It was relief. She blinked and sat up. "But I've been here all the time."

She looked at her watch and was surprised to see that it was well past midnight.

David sat down beside her on the couch. "Then why didn't you tell somebody? I thought you'd gone to bed upstairs, but when I went up, you weren't there. The bed hadn't even been turned down. I searched the whole house before I remembered this room. The door was closed and everything was dark—"

He turned toward her, and the relief in his eyes was rapidly turning to anger. "I was about to organize a search party to track you through the woods." His hands gripped her shoulders, and he shook her as he said, "Damn you, were you deliberately hiding from me?"

Robyn clutched at his arms, trying to make him stop shaking her. "No, David! I had no idea you'd worry about me. I thought you and Joyce would want to use that room."

He stopped shaking her and glared. "Joyce and me? Fat chance. I've been too busy tracking you down to concentrate on the subtleties of lovemaking."

Robyn could feel her own temper rising. "What a shame! I'm sure Joyce was sorely disappointed. The way you were pawing her left no doubt about your intentions."

"Pawing her!" David roared. "I never 'paw' any

woman!" He stood and yanked her up with him. "Go to bed. I've lost enough sleep over you for one night."

She pulled away from him and stood her ground. "No, I'm not going to sleep in your room. I'll sleep right here on the couch."

He gave her a look of exasperation and without warning swept her up in his arms and headed toward the staircase. She threw her arms around his neck for balance and hissed, "Put me down."

He paid no attention to her protests as he carried her up the stairs and down the hall to his room where he dumped her unceremoniously on her bed. She started to jump up, but he pushed her back, gently but firmly. "Now," he said in a no-nonsense tone, "I don't want any more trouble from you tonight."

He took his pajama trousers out of the drawer and turned to her. "Are you going to lie quietly while I go into the bathroom to change, or do I have to undress right here?"

She knew he would, too. She settled back on the bed and said, "I'll stay here. I promise."

As soon as he was gone, she crawled in between the sheets. A short time later, he came back dressed in his pajama trousers and gathered up a change of clean clothes from drawers and closets.

She snuggled deeper under the covers and said, "David, I'm sorry I frightened you."

For a minute he just looked at her; then he walked over and sat on the side of her bed. He took her face in his hands and kissed her firmly on the lips. "Don't you ever do that to me again," he murmured, then stood and walked out the door, shutting it softly behind him.

* * *

David was gone when Robyn got up the next morning, but he returned at ten o'clock with the news that the road was cleared and they could go back to Boulder. Robyn was both relieved and apprehensive. Relieved because she couldn't stand much more of the tension and distrust that radiated between her and the other members of the household and apprehensive because she had no idea what David intended to do about her once they were back in town. Would he press charges against her, or would he let the matter drop?

Everyone was busy getting ready to leave, but since Robyn had nothing to take but her purse, she decided to go out and inspect her car. David had moved it out of the road and onto the wide driveway where the other vehicles were kept and had issued orders that she was not to go near it.

Now, however, she was going to have to drive it back to Boulder, and she had to know if it was in running order. Obviously, it was or David couldn't have moved it, but without her glasses and with the car being damaged, she was nervous about starting out in it. Thank goodness it was only about fifteen miles into town.

She walked around the red Pinto, but except for the broken headlight, it seemed to be in good shape. A lot better than poor little Shelley! Robyn searched her purse for her keys and then remembered she hadn't seen them since the accident. Hadn't even thought of them.

David obviously must have them, since he'd driven the car into the driveway. She turned to go back to the house when she saw him coming toward her. He stopped in front of her and held out his hand, the keys dangling from his fingers. "Were you looking for these?" he asked, his tone friendly but cool.

"Yes, thank you." She reached for them, but he selected one and unlocked the car door next to her, then walked around and unlocked the other one.

Again, she held out her hand, but he ignored her and put the ring of keys back in his pocket. "I'll drive your car back to town. Joyce can drive mine."

She felt resentment rising in her. "I can drive my own car, thank you," she said. "If you'll just give me the keys." Again, she held out her hand.

David shook his head and gave her a look of disgust. "I can't tell how extensively your car is damaged, and you've admitted you can't see to drive without your glasses. I'm not going to turn you loose on the highway under those conditions. After what you did to Shelley, I should think you'd have a little concern for the other people on the road."

Robyn's temper flared. "I did not hit Shelley! I wasn't even driving the car that night! Now give me my keys. I'm perfectly capable of driving my own car."

His face hardened, and his eyes flashed fire. "Why don't you grow up, Robyn, and admit the truth? I'm sick to death of your lies. Now you can either ride back to Boulder with me or walk, but you're not driving this car!" He stalked back to the house, leaving her standing there gaping.

The ride back to Boulder was made in silence. Robyn slouched in her seat, her chin sunk on her chest and a scowl creasing her bruised face. David's hands clenched the steering wheel, and he focused all his attention on the road. On the outskirts of the city he asked for her address, and she told him. He drove right to it and parked on the street in front of the old

Victorian structure that had been converted into a boarding house.

So this was it, the moment of truth. Four days ago at this time, she'd never heard of Dr. David Christopher. Now the thought that she might never see him again was one she didn't want to face. How could four short days turn a person's life around so completely?

She twisted in her seat and faced David, who was sitting quietly staring straight ahead. Her voice was low and hesitant as she said, "Good-by, David. I—I'm truly sorry we had to meet under such tragic circumstances. I'll be here at least until September if you decide to press charges against me, but please, will you let Irene keep me informed on how Shelley is recovering? It's really very important to me."

He said nothing, but opened the door and got out of the car. She watched as he walked around and opened her door. He helped her alight, then took her arm to lead her to the house.

"It's not necessary for you to come up with me," she protested. "I'm sure Joyce will be along any minute with your car to pick you up."

He marched her along as he said, "I'm coming up to help you pack."

"Pack!" she screeched.

"That's right. You're going to pack your clothes and come home with me."

Robyn could only stare at him. "Oh no, I'm not," she snapped as he unlocked the door to her room.

She was relieved to see that the room was clean and neat, and empty. Her roommate usually left her things strung all over the place.

David followed her in and shut the door behind them. "It's either that or go to jail," he said.

Robyn's legs gave way, and she slumped down on the side of the bed. Of course. She should have known he wasn't through tormenting her yet.

She looked up at him, her eyes wide with apprehension, but he wasn't impressed. "You had been drinking and speeding when your car hit my daughter. It's a miracle she wasn't killed, and I'm not going to release you to do the same thing to someone else. You're a transient, a gypsy with no permanent address in Boulder or anywhere else, and you're not going to get away from me until I'm sure Shelley has suffered no lasting damage."

He walked away from her and opened the closet door. "I'm also going to see to it that you enroll in a rehabilitation program where they will teach you to drive carefully. If we're fortunate, they may also teach you to tell the truth."

"Rehabilitation!" Robyn practically yelled the word as he began removing her dresses and blouses, complete with hangers, from the closet.

This had to be a nightmare, Robyn thought, one of those terrifyingly real ones that cause you to wake up screaming. But why didn't she wake up?

She couldn't move into David's home and live with him! Not because she didn't trust him but because she didn't trust herself. No matter how cold, angry or sarcastic he was to her, the minute he smiled and touched her, she melted. She couldn't help it. If she was this susceptible to him after less than a week, what would she be like after a whole summer in his intimate presence?

She shuddered. She'd be lost. Totally, irrevocably lost. The next time he took her in his arms and kissed her the way he had in the woods, she'd let him do anything he wanted with her. And afterward she'd be his forever whether he wanted her or not. There was the snag, because he'd made it clear that he didn't want her, not on a permanent basis.

She made one last desperate effort to change his mind. "Does Joyce live with you?" she asked as she packed underwear in one of her blue suitcases.

David was packing shoes in another case. "Of course not," he grated. "She has an apartment out near the college. What kind of a father do you think I am? I'd never subject Shelley to a series of live-in 'aunties.'"

"Then what's Shelley going to think when I move in?" There was a note of triumph in her voice.

David merely glanced at her. "She'll have no cause to think you're anything but the temporary houseguest you are. You'll sleep on the second floor across from Shelley's and Irene's rooms. The master suite is on the first floor, and I have no intentions of climbing those stairs to come to you. You needn't worry, Robyn. I have no designs on your virtue."

Robyn was appalled to discover that she felt disappointment rather than relief.

Robyn's reception at David's house was varied and anything but placid. Irene seemed puzzled but pleased. Joyce was furious and went storming next door to tell her sister. Eve was disgusted, and Graham was amused. Shelley—when David brought her home from the hospital after lunch—was the only one who was genuinely delighted.

The Christopher home was a large redwood and brick two-story structure set in an acre of huge old shade trees, colorful flower gardens and a thick green

lawn. The garden was carried inside where the double-
door entry led to a planted and sky-lit atrium that
provided a peaceful setting for the dining and living
rooms that opened onto it. Robyn peeked into both
rooms, and was delighted with what she saw.

The dining room was highlighted by a high, open-
beamed ceiling and recessed spotlights, and the dark,
richly polished table could easily seat ten without extra
leaves. The living room on the other side of the wall
was only slightly less open. Red was the predominant
color in the woven draperies, the Chippendale sofa and
in a ten-foot-long tapestry that hung next to the massive
rock fireplace. The oak parquet floors were highly
polished and provided a rich background for the Oriental rugs.

Irene later took Robyn on a tour of the house, which
featured a spacious gourmet-pleasing kitchen in the
back of the house, with imported ceramic tile, built-in
cabinets and a big, informal eating area. Across the hall
was a small den with walls of books and a fireplace. As
David had indicated, the master bedroom suite, con-
sisting of two rooms and a bath, took up most of the
north wing. Irene did not take Robyn into those rooms
and allowed her only a quick glimpse from the doorway
of David's bedroom. She had time to notice a breath-
taking view of the mountains from a glass wall, another
smaller fireplace and a king-size bed. Apparently,
David's ex-wife had no objection to sleeping with him
here at home.

Up the stairway leading from one end of the living
room, Robyn was shown to her room on the second
floor. Tastefully decorated in shades of blue, it was light
and spacious with a view of the gardens. The furnishings were sleek and contemporary, and the headboard

on the bed was covered in the same quilted blue and white material as the spread. She shared a bath with the unoccupied room next door, similar to hers but decorated in yellow and lime.

Across the hall were Shelley's and Irene's rooms, which were side by side and connected by a bath. It was a luxurious, well-cared-for home that bespoke of wealth and breeding.

Robyn had called the box office from the cabin earlier that morning and left a message for Tyler Kerr, her director, explaining about the accident and the rock slide and telling him she probably wouldn't be back to start rehearsals until the following day. The story sounded so melodramatic that she knew he wouldn't believe it and would deliver one of his famous tongue-lashings when she finally did show up. She was in no hurry to endure that, so although she could have gone to the theater after lunch, she decided to stay home and entertain Shelley while David spent the afternoon at the animal hospital.

Shelley's leg was encased in a walking cast, but she'd been instructed to stay off it as much as possible for the next few days. Irene made her a bed on the couch in the living room where she could watch the big-screen color television set when she wasn't playing games with Robyn.

When David came home at dinner time, he brought with him a small, black, curly-haired cockapoo to replace the dog that had been lost in the rock slide. Shelley was overjoyed with the white-faced puppy, and after dinner, Robyn excused herself and went to her room so that David could have some time alone with his daughter.

*   *   *

Robyn was up at dawn the next morning, excited at the prospect of starting rehearsals and apprehensive at the thought of facing Tyler Kerr's wrath because she had missed the first day. She dressed in jeans, sneakers and a camellia-pink pullover terry top. Her forehead and cheek were still discolored and her eye slightly swollen, but she decided against wearing makeup other than lipstick. She would need the visible evidence of her accident to substantiate her improbable story of why she didn't show up at the tent yesterday.

Downstairs she busied herself in the kitchen making coffee and searching the refrigerator for bacon and eggs since Irene hadn't come down yet. She was whipping eggs for an omelet when she heard the door open behind her and turned, expecting Irene. It was David, and from the surprised look on his face, she knew he'd expected Irene, too.

He grinned and sniffed the air. "Mmm, something smells good. You startled me, Robyn. I didn't recognize you at first in those clothes."

His gaze ran over her slowly and lingered on the curve of her derriere in the snug jeans before traveling up to the less obvious swell of her full breasts under the loose pullover. "You look different, younger, less sophisticated."

She nodded in agreement. "I know. I'm going to get rid of that jump suit as quickly as I can. I can't stand the sight of it after—" She paused and changed the subject. "How many eggs do you want in your omelet?"

"You're not only decorative but useful." He walked over to the cupboard and took down a colorful glass before answering her question. "Three, please. Is there any orange juice in the frig?"

She poured the egg mixture into the hot skillet. "Yes," she said, "but it's frozen. Do you know how to mix it?"

"Of course I know how to mix it," he grumbled playfully. "I was probably cooking before you were born."

For some reason, she wasn't amused. "I told you, I'm not a child."

The teasing look in his eyes disappeared. "No, you're not, are you? Your appearance is deceiving."

They worked together in silence until breakfast was ready. Then David seated her and sat down beside her at the round oak table. When he spoke, it was on an entirely different subject. "Are you wearing your contact lenses?"

She shook her head. "No, my eye is still puffy. Since I travel around so much, I carry my eyeglasses prescription with me. I'll stop at an oculist's and see if I can get a rush job on a new pair."

"Meanwhile, how are you going to get back and forth to rehearsals?"

She looked at him, surprised. "I'll drive, of course. I'm not blind, you know."

"After what you did to Shelley, you couldn't prove it by me." His voice was gruff, cold. "You're not driving anywhere until you get new glasses, and you're not driving your car until it's thoroughly checked for damage and the headlight is fixed."

Robyn threw her napkin down on the table and glared at him. "It's my car, and I'll drive it anytime I please, with or without my glasses!"

He put down his fork and glared right back at her. "Don't push your luck, Robyn. I made it plain that I intend to see that you learn to drive safely. That includes not driving a damaged car without your glasses. You're obviously totally irresponsible, and if you don't follow my instructions, I'll have your driver's license taken away. Now what time do you have to be at rehearsals?"

She was too shocked by his outburst to protest. Instead, she murmured weakly, "Nine o'clock."

He looked at his watch. "I have an eight-thirty appointment, so I can't wait around to take you to the tent, but I'll have my gardener, Will Otto, drive you over. Call the house when you're ready to come home and someone will pick you up."

He stood and pushed back his chair just as Robyn found her voice. "You—you—" She couldn't think of a name nasty enough to call him. "There's no way you can keep me from driving my own car."

He walked away, but when he got to the door, he turned and looked at her with a hard, level gaze. "Oh, yes, there is. I still have your keys."

Robyn stared, impotent with fury as he strode out of the room.

Will Otto was a man of few words, and he apparently reserved them for special occasions. When Irene introduced him to Robyn, he merely touched his cap and helped her into the long gray Cadillac. He answered her attempts at conversation as they drove along with either *ja* or *nein,* although she was sure he spoke English. He wasn't unfriendly, just not talkative. When they got to the tent, he helped her out of the car, touched his cap again and drove off.

Robyn stood in front of the huge, sprawling, green and white striped tent, trying to gather enough courage to face the brilliant but explosive director. Once that was out of the way, she would look for the man who had been driving her car the night of the accident. Would he be here? He had to be! He wouldn't have been at the cocktail party if he hadn't been connected in some way with the musicals.

She went through the wide main entrance and started down the dirt aisle to the round stage in the center of the round tent. It was like a mammoth pie, she thought, with aisles at regularly spaced intervals that marked off the pieces. During the performance, the actors, singers and dancers used these aisles to get to and from the stage, involving the audience in the process, making them not only observers but participants, and they loved it.

As she approached the stage, Robyn realized that there was a man sprawled in the lone chair on the otherwise-empty platform. He was a small man, not much taller than she, and slender, with sandy hair and light-blue eyes that watched her as she moved toward him.

When she got close enough to hear, Tyler Kerr spoke. "Well, well, if it isn't—uh—Robyn?—Robyn Flannery, come at last to grace us with her presence. The rest of us worked our butts off yesterday, but I understand you were vacationing in the mountains and just couldn't tear yourself away."

Robyn cringed at his sarcasm and tried to explain. "Please, Tyler, it wasn't like that. I told you, I was—"

She'd walked across the stage and was standing in front of him when his voice cut through her sentence. "Good heavens, what happened to you?" He was looking at her bruised face. "You can't seriously consider going on stage like that?"

"The discoloration will be mostly faded by Monday,

and pancake makeup will hide what's left," she replied. "I told you I was involved in a car accident, and then a rock slide cut off the access road to the highway. They even had to fly the little girl who was injured out in a helicopter."

She had him off guard and intended to press her advantage. "I'm sorry I missed rehearsals yesterday, but the operetta we're doing has been around for so long that I know the music by heart, and I'll pick up on the dances fast, you'll see. I am, after all, a professional."

Tyler Kerr nodded but made no reply.

The morning was hectic. Robyn didn't see the man from the party and had no time to look for him. With only a week to rehearse before opening night, there was no time to waste, and after this week, it would be even worse. As usual with summer stock, each show ran for a week then was replaced by another, so once the season started, they would rehearse the following week's operetta during the day and give the current performance at night. That they were all well-known classic musicals made it easier.

Robyn took advantage of the lunch break to talk to as many people as she could and ask about the man at the party. In trying to keep her inquiry low key, she intimated that he was a stranger who interested her and that she wanted to see him again. She didn't want the real reason made known yet. All these people knew was that she had been involved in an accident on the way home from Nederland after the party and had been stranded in the mountains for a few days.

The problem was that when she began describing the man, she realized that the description fit half the men in

Boulder. Medium height, medium weight, medium coloring. She couldn't even remember exactly what he'd been wearing. Light shirt and dark slacks, but she'd been so upset by the spilled drink, the broken glasses and the approaching storm that she didn't notice the colors.

The afternoon was as hectic as the morning, but Robyn used the short breaks to talk to the crew, the electricians, hairdressers, makeup and wardrobe people, but still to no avail. A few of them thought they knew who she was looking for, but when the man was pointed out to her, he proved to be the wrong one.

By the end of the day, Robyn was exhausted, but she wasn't going to give David the satisfaction of calling him to pick her up. She took a bus instead. He wasn't home yet when she got there, and Shelley was napping, so Robyn took a hot, fragrant, leisurely bath to help relax some of the knots in her muscles. She slipped into clean panties and bra and glanced at the bed. It looked so soft and inviting, and she'd been up since daybreak. Dinner wouldn't be served for an hour; she had time to lie down and rest for a few minutes. . . .

A knock penetrated the outer reaches of her awareness, but it had nothing to do with her, and she burrowed deeper into the down-filled pillow. Another knock and then someone calling her name. She knew she should answer, but she couldn't seem to put her mind to it.

It was the hand on her forehead that brought her fully awake, and she rolled over and opened her eyes to find David bending over her, a look of concern on his face. The concern was echoed in his voice as he said, "Robyn, are you all right?"

She must have been awfully sound asleep because

she was still disoriented, but she liked the feel of his hand against her skin. She blinked. "David? I was asleep. Hey, I know this is your house, but surely I'm entitled to a little privacy. Don't you ever knock before entering a lady's bedroom?"

He pulled the bench from the dressing table to the side of the bed and sat down. "I did knock. I also called to you. When you didn't answer, I was afraid . . ."

He gently brushed the auburn curls from the side of her face and examined the bruise. "I want you to see a doctor. That bash on the head was a hard one, and I'm not qualified to diagnose the extent of your injury. I'm afraid I was so upset over Shelley that I've neglected you shamefully. I should have taken you to the hospital along with her. Do you know a doctor here in Boulder?"

Robyn shook her head. "No, but I'm fine, really. It's not unusual for me to be exhausted at the end of a day of rehearsals. I don't think you realize how much physical exertion goes into those dances we do, and when we go over them again and again all day long—well, until I build up a little more stamina, I may sleep through dinner every night."

He continued to caress her cheek absently. "Nevertheless, I'll make an appointment with my family doctor for you tomorrow. You should be examined by someone more qualified than me. Oh, yes, I had Will take your car into the garage this morning. They'll call you with an estimate. Did you leave your glasses prescription with an oculist?"

His caress was doing disturbingly pleasant things to her, and Robyn wondered what David would do if she put her hand on his temptingly close knee. She pushed aside the thought and answered, "No, I forgot. I was so tired after rehearsing all day that I came right home."

He stopped caressing her face and pulled the bed sheet up around her shoulders. It was only then that she realized, to her embarrassment, that she had been lying there uncovered from the waist up, with nothing on but a lacy bra. She could feel the hot color flood her face as she belatedly clutched the sheet under her chin.

David grinned. "Sorry about that, but I'm only human. Another few minutes and I'd have forgotten my reason for coming up here, which was to tell you dinner is ready. Of course, if you're not hungry, we could—"

"But I am hungry!" She glared at him as she sat up, pulling the sheet with her. "And if you were a gentleman, you wouldn't come bursting into my room when I'm asleep and—uh—exposed. Now get out of here and let me get dressed."

He laughed with undisguised amusement as he stood. "Yes, ma'am, but you'll have to admit I acted with admirable restraint."

Robyn threw a pillow at him just as he stepped out of the room and closed the door behind him.

The following day, Wednesday, Robyn got a clean bill of health from David's doctor and then continued her quest for the mysterious stranger. She talked to the director and the casting agent and asked if any of the people who had originally been hired had either resigned or been fired. None had.

On Thursday, she decided the man may have been the husband or boy friend of one of the women in the cast or crew, so she spent all day being friendly and asking questions. By this time, she was well acquainted with her coworkers but still had no luck. Only two of the girls were married, and both of their husbands had worked on the day of the party, so they hadn't been able to go. Four more had taken boy friends, but on further questioning, she found out that two of the men were blonds, one a redhead and one a brunet. All were tall and handsome, the kind who would stand out in a crowd.

Things weren't going well at David's house, either. She and Shelley had formed a close, loving relationship, but David remained an enigma, friendly one moment, distant the next. He'd continued in the teasing mood Wednesday evening as they'd played with Shelley, but Thursday he'd come home with her repaired automobile and the announcement that he'd made arrangements for her to attend a rehabilitation class for drunken drivers.

Robyn was furious. "I will not attend a class with a lot of drunks!" she'd squealed. "I've never been drunk in my life, and I was not driving the car when it hit Shelley. If you'd listen to me and start looking for that man—"

David swore and banged his hand on the table. "Will you forget that idiotic story and face the truth for once! I'm not going to run off chasing phantoms. I'm trying to help you, but I've about run out of patience. I hate to sound like a broken record, but it's either go to the classes or to jail."

She'd wanted to hit him, throw something, stamp her feet and scream. Instead, she'd turned and run upstairs to her room. Later, Irene took her dinner up on a tray, but she was too upset to eat.

The next morning, Friday, she and David breakfasted in silence, and then David, who would still not give her her car keys, drove her to the tent. As soon as he stopped, she started to get out, but he caught her by the wrist and pulled her back. He sounded tired, discouraged, as he said, "I'm serious about this, Robyn, so you might as well accept it and start attending those classes. You won't get your keys back until you do. It's only an hour a day for five days, and you can choose either mornings or evenings."

She jerked her wrist from his grasp and mimicked, "Only an hour a day. And just where am I supposed to find that hour? Starting Monday, we'll be giving a performance every night and rehearsing the following week's show all day. I don't even have a whole hour for lunch. Of course, I suppose I could skip dinner—"

"Don't talk nonsense," David snapped. "You won't be skipping any meals. Are you telling me you'll be working all day and half the night for the rest of the summer?"

"That's exactly what I'm telling you," she said in a curt, biting tone as she opened the door and jumped out of the car before he could stop her.

That day, Robyn concentrated her questioning on the orchestra. Had any of the men invited a friend or relative to the cocktail party? Had any of the women brought a husband or boy friend? Nothing. The man, whoever he was, had simply dropped off the face of the earth!

Tyler Kerr asked the cast to return after dinner that night for a short session with the lights. David grumbled about slave labor but drove Robyn back and stayed until she was finished. In the car on the way home, she curled up on the seat beside him and was nearly asleep by the time they turned into the driveway. It was eleven o'clock.

He helped her out of the car and led her into the dimly lit living room. He sat her on the couch and told her to stay there, then disappeared, only to reappear in a few minutes bearing two highballs. He handed one to Robyn as he sat down beside her. "Drink that," he said. "You're nearly out on your feet. That egomaniac you call a director has no right to work you such long hours. It's against the law among other things."

Robyn took a sip of the smooth, cool drink. It was big enough and strong enough to last her all night. She sighed and leaned back. "It's not all that bad. After all, it only lasts seven weeks. Then we're free to relax all year if we can afford it. Besides"—she grinned—"all that dancing is good for the figure."

His face was shadowed in the dim light, but she could feel his gaze on her, and his voice was soft as he said, "If your figure were any better, it would drive me clear out of my mind."

He put his drink down and took her into his arms. Robyn had no intention of resisting as she snuggled into his embrace, also setting her drink down. David's breath was warm on her face as his cheek rubbed against hers, and his lips caressed her temple and nibbled at her ear lobe.

She shivered with pleasure as he continued on to nuzzle the sensitive hollow at the side of her neck. His hand cupped her breast through her thin cotton shirt. She twined her fingers in his thick, blond hair, and he moved his head just enough to murmur close to her ear. "Robyn, I swear you've cast a spell on me. I can't keep my hands off you and that's the truth. I've wanted to hold you like this so badly for so long."

She stroked his hair and whispered, "I thought you didn't like me."

He lifted his head and looked down at her, his green eyes dark with emotion. "Oh, I like you, believe me I do. I like your radiant smile and the breathless quality of your voice when you're excited. I like the way your deep-blue eyes soften when you look at Shelley and your quick compassion. I like the way you touch me and the way you respond when I touch you."

His hands were moving restlessly over her, exploring, caressing, learning. "I like the way your body feels pressed against mine, and I like the fresh, sweet taste of your mouth when I kiss you, like this."

His lips moved over hers lightly, teasingly, then pressed against them insistently. Little pinpricks of fire licked at Robyn's nerve endings as she wound her arms around his neck and allowed her own lips to part and savor his probing tongue. They both shifted so that their bodies meshed, and the pinpricks of fire became flame as she felt his hard, driving need for her.

David moved back slightly so that he was speaking against the corner of her mouth, and his voice was husky with desire as he said, "Robyn, oh, Robyn, I can't control my feelings for you. First I tried to ignore them, then I denied them, but it's no use. I want you, need you, I—"

With a low moan, his mouth once more claimed hers, and he lifted her across his lap, pulling her shirt free from her jeans so that he could touch the bare flesh underneath. Robyn's arms tightened around him, and she cuddled closer as he unfastened her bra and took possession of her taut, round breasts.

They were so engrossed in each other that they heard nothing until a clear, melodious voice cut through the silence. "Well really, darling, I thought you were too old for groping around on the sofa like a teenager! If I'd known you were so intimately occupied, I'd have rung the bell instead of using my key."

David and Robyn tore apart, shocked and dismayed at the unwanted interruption, and David bounded to his feet as he stared at the gorgeous silvery blonde in the archway.

His voice was rough with frustration and surprise as he gasped, "Belinda!"

Their unexpected guest was Belinda Christopher, Shelley's mother and David's ex-wife, the woman Robyn had good reason to believe he was still in love with!

Chapter Six

Robyn felt like a teenager who'd been caught by her mother making out under the bushes with her boy friend. She was hotly embarrassed and coldly furious. How could she have succumbed so rapidly and so completely to David? And why was this woman who was no longer a member of the household allowed to wander in without even the courtesy of a knock?

They were stupid questions, she knew. She'd responded to David's lovemaking because she wanted him as badly as he wanted her and she couldn't resist him. His ex-wife retained her key and her live-in privileges because she was stunningly beautiful, smolderingly sensual, and David loved her so much that he'd take her any time she'd come to him. Robyn felt debased.

The pregnant silence lasted only a few seconds, but it seemed like an eternity to Robyn as she knelt on the couch, disheveled and no doubt looking as frustrated as she felt. David stood motionless, apparently trying to gather his wits about him and think of something to say.

Belinda was the only one in control of the situation. Like the actress she was, she made the most of her entrance as she stood, tall and commanding, in the glow of the hall light. Her luscious body was dressed in a gray silk suit that matched her eyes. The full A-line skirt swirled around her nicely curved calves and directed attention to the delicate gray sandals that buckled around her slender ankles. Her shimmering silver hair fell in a soft flip around her shoulders, giving her an ethereal look, like a displaced angel.

David was the first to recover, but he couldn't disguise his shock as he said, "Belinda, what are you doing here?"

She walked slowly toward him. "I've come to see my poor injured daughter, of course. Really, darling, I expected you to take better care of her."

Before David could answer, she put her arms around his neck and kissed him, leisurely and thoroughly. His arms closed around her waist, and Robyn, rooted to the couch, closed her eyes to shut out the taunting scene.

She opened them again when she heard Belinda's low, throaty laugh and saw that the other woman had pulled away from David and was now looking at her, although she continued to speak to David. "I'm sorry if I blundered in at a crucial moment, but how was I to know you've taken to bringing your one-night stands home? I understood you kept an apartment for that sort of thing."

Robyn cringed and opened her mouth to do something, probably scream, when David's voice stopped her. "Knock it off, Belinda!" He reached down and took Robyn's hands, bringing her to her feet beside him. "This is Robyn Flannery. Robyn, Shelley's mother, Belinda." His hand squeezed Robyn's, who was trembling noticeably. "Robyn is a houseguest."

Robyn saw a flash of anger flit across David's ex-wife's exquisite face before she quickly erased it. "Oh, well, in that case, maybe I should have a talk with Graham. I thought we'd agreed that if you had custody of Shelley, you wouldn't subject her to a parade of your live-in playmates. I won't tolerate it."

Robyn turned blindly and tried to leave, but David caught her around the waist and held her to him. His voice was harsh with controlled fury as he said, "We had no such agreement because we both knew it wasn't necessary. Robyn is just what I said, a guest, and you owe her an apology."

Belinda shrugged. "I find that hard to believe after the scene I walked in on just now. Good heavens, David, I'm not stupid, and my eyesight is excellent even in this romantic light."

A hot flush of shame and resentment coursed through Robyn, and again she tried to leave, but the arm that held her tightened.

Belinda apparently realized she was losing the advantage she'd gained by her sudden appearance. She dropped her sarcastic tone and purred, "Sorry, darling, I didn't mean to embarrass your little friend—uh—Robyn, isn't it? You two go right ahead with what you were doing. I'm going to bed." She looked meaningfully at David. "I'll see you later. Please bring my suitcases when you come. For now, I'll use one of the nightgowns I left in our room last time I was here."

She walked out of the living room, and Robyn could hear her spike heels clicking on the highly polished parquet floor as she walked to the master bedroom suite.

Robyn looked up into David's white, set face and muttered, "If you don't let me go, I'm going to scream for help. I guarantee it will bring Irene and Shelley running."

His grasp on her loosened, and she twisted away from him and stumbled out of the room. Behind her David called, "Robyn, please, I—"

Whatever it was he wanted to say, she didn't want to hear, and she ran up the stairs to the safety of her room and locked the door.

It was a long night, and Robyn spent most of it pacing, too wrought up to sleep. Her tormenting thoughts went around and around, starting with—Why did I make the colossal mistake of falling in love with the one man who can never love me?—and ending with—What am I going to do now?

She'd given up trying to deceive herself. She knew she loved David, had probably been in love with him from the moment he swept her into his arms and carried her from her car to his cabin. But what was she going to do about it? One thing was certain, she couldn't stay in his house any longer. Not with Belinda sleeping in his bed downstairs!

She winced as the picture of them entwined in each other's arms on the king-size bed in the master bedroom intruded into her mind. Of course, she had no way of knowing for certain that's what they were doing, but Belinda had made it plain that they would be sleeping together, and David hadn't denied it.

Toward morning, Robyn dozed, but a steady procession of vague, disturbing dreams kept her tossing and turning until finally, at seven-thirty, she got up and dressed, although she didn't have to report in at the tent until after lunch. This morning, Tyler was rehearsing the two stars of the performance without the chorus.

It was sunny and warm, a beautiful morning, and Robyn dressed in a wrap-around denim skirt and a sleeveless red plaid shirt. It would be an exercise in futility to try to compete in the glamour department with Belinda, and she wasn't going to waste her time.

In the kitchen, Irene greeted her cheerfully, then took a good look at her and sobered. "What's the matter with you?" she demanded. "Are you sick? You're so pale, and you have dark circles under your eyes. If you ask me, I think you're working too hard. It's about time they gave you a few hours off. Why don't you go back to bed and I'll bring your breakfast up?"

The housekeeper's concern warmed Robyn, but she shook her head and poured herself a cup of coffee. "Thanks, Irene, but I'm okay. I just had a little trouble sleeping last night."

She took her coffee to the table and sat down just as the door opened and Belinda, dressed in a black lace peignoir that played peekaboo with a black satin night-gown, glided through the door, a radiant smile on her face. Robyn almost spilled her coffee.

Irene was nearly as surprised as Robyn and David had been last night. "Mrs. Christopher!" she rasped. "Where did you come from? When did you get in?"

"Hello, Irene," Belinda greeted her. "I got in late last night. You're looking well. I hope you've been taking good care of Dr. Christopher while I've been gone."

"Didn't I always?" Irene sniffed, apparently more surprised than pleased to see her employer's ex-wife.

Belinda ignored the remark and turned her attention

to Robyn. "Good morning—uh—Robyn," she said, then stared, noticing the fading bruises on Robyn's face for the first time. "What happened to you? Don't tell me David beats you?"

Robyn was just about to hurl the cup of steaming coffee at her when, fortunately for them both, Shelley came in. She stopped, her gray-green eyes wide with surprise as she cried, "Mommie!" and limped awkwardly over to her mother. She threw her arms around Belinda, and her mother hugged her but complained, "Shelley, do be careful. Don't brush me with that heavy cast. You'll tear my new peignoir."

Shelley drew away, crestfallen. "I—I'm sorry."

Robyn wondered if she could still throw the coffee at Belinda. The witch! She hadn't seen her daughter in months, and Shelley had been injured, could easily have been killed, but all Belinda could think of was keeping the child at a distance so she wouldn't get mussed. The disappointment in Shelley's eyes was heartbreaking, and Robyn had just started to reach out to her when Belinda apparently realized what Robyn intended and quickly put her arms around her daughter. "It's all right, honey," she said sweetly. "You just took me by surprise. Come on, let's take daddy a cup of coffee. He's still in bed." She winked suggestively at Robyn. "Poor David didn't get much sleep last night. It was quite evident he'd missed me."

Belinda took the placated child by the hand and led her toward the master bedroom suite, and this time Robyn did spill her coffee. It splashed over the table and dripped off the sides as Robyn hunched over, sick from the blow she'd been dealt.

Irene came to the rescue with a sponge, and Robyn

escaped out the kitchen door, down the steps and across the terraced gardens to a gazebo that was partially hidden from the house by a cluster of fragrant, blooming lilac bushes. The door was unlocked, and she went inside and sank down on a lacy white wrought-iron bench. She dropped her head in her hands and sat there silently, willing herself not to cry. She'd had enough of that in the mountains. If she could only pull herself together so she could think!

She'd been there no more than two or three minutes when she heard the door open and looked up, praying it wasn't someone from the house. It was Graham. "I was coming through the hedge to beg a cup of coffee from you when I saw you come in here," he said. He paused, then crossed the floor in two strides taking both her hands in his and searching her face. "Robyn, good Lord, what's the matter? You're pale as a ghost, and you look ill. Has David done this to you?"

Robyn shook her head and lowered her eyes. "No, not really. Oh, Graham—"

Her voice broke, and he gathered her in his arms and cradled her against him, rocking her ever so slightly. "Baby, baby," he crooned. "Tell papa."

She buried her face in his shoulder. The soft cashmere of his sweater tickled her cheek, and the elusive scent of shaving lotion was clean and fresh. Graham was a genuinely nice man, and she knew she could confide in him and he would keep her secrets.

Her voice was muffled against his sweater as she said, "Mrs. Christopher is here."

Graham stiffened. "Mrs. Christopher? You mean Belinda?" He swore softly. "When did she come, and what does she want now?"

"She came late last night," Robyn answered. "She didn't ring the bell or anything, just walked in. David and I were—were in the living room and—and—"

She paused, tongue-tied and wondering how to proceed, but it wasn't necessary. Graham understood. "You mean she caught you and David making love on the couch?" He rolled his eyes. "Yi, yi, yi! Why didn't the idiot take you into his bedroom?"

Robyn pulled away from him. "Oh, no, Graham, it wasn't like that. He was just—just kissing me. We weren't—I mean we hadn't—"

"You mean she walked in just as things were getting too hot to control." He shook his head in dismay. "As I remember, something like that happened up at the cabin, too." An impish grin quivered at the corners of his mouth. "Poor Dave! If this happens with any degree of regularity, you're going to unman him, honey."

"Me!" Robyn squealed. "It's not my fault, and you needn't feel sorry for David! He got what he was after, but it was Belinda he took to bed, not me."

Graham looked genuinely shocked. "You're kidding! He slept with Belinda after—I don't believe it!"

Robyn's temper had finally asserted itself. "Then ask her. She'll be only too happy to tell you. She's been flaunting it to everyone else this morning."

Robyn stood and looked out the glass wall that faced Graham and Eve's garden. Her hands were clenched at her sides, and her voice was taut. "I've got to get away from here, Graham. I can't live in the same house with that woman, and I'm sure that now David will be happy to let me go."

Graham came to stand beside her. "I'm not at all sure what's going on here, but I agree that you can't stay under these circumstances. Do you have some-place else to go?"

She nodded. "Yes, I can go back to the rooming house."

He took her arm. "Come on. We'll face David and Belinda together. If he gives you any trouble, I'll remind him of a few legal facts he's been ignoring."

The couple in question were sitting at the kitchen table when Graham and Robyn came in. Belinda was still in her sexy black peignoir, but she'd lost most of the triumphant exuberance she'd displayed earlier. David was very inelegantly attired in blue jeans and a white T-shirt, and he looked bleary-eyed and grumpy. Not at all the way a man is supposed to look after a night of ecstasy.

He frowned as he glanced at the two standing just inside the doorway arm in arm. Then his attention settled on Robyn, and he asked, "Where have you been? I've been looking for you."

She was surprised that he'd given her a thought. "I went for a walk and met Graham."

"So I see," David muttered. "Do you two make a habit of meeting like this?"

Robyn's head snapped up, but it was Graham who answered. "I'll overlook that remark, chum, since you seem to have taken on more than you can handle." He nodded toward Belinda. "Hello, Belinda. I heard you were here."

Belinda shrugged. "Obviously. Hi, Graham. Does Eve know you're sharing Robyn with David?"

Robyn stiffened, but Graham patted her hand and kept his voice cool and taunting. "If she doesn't, I'm sure you'll tell her. Now can we all stop sniping at each other and try to behave in a civilized manner? Robyn has something to say."

David pushed his chair back and stood. "And I want to talk to her, *alone*. Why don't you and Belinda keep each other company while Robyn and I—"

Robyn didn't want to be alone with David, and she tightened her hold on Graham's arm. He understood the signal and said, "Sit down, Dave. This is going to be a general meeting."

He pulled out a chair at the table for Robyn, then seated himself. David sat down reluctantly and growled, "Since when are you giving me orders in my own house?"

"Since you began mistreating Robyn."

David glared. "Is that what she told you?"

Graham's cool was heating up. "You've got one more woman than the law allows, and Robyn's leaving."

David straightened in his chair. "What in hell are you talking about?"

This time Robyn spoke for herself. "I think you know by now that I'm serious about honoring my contract with the theater-in-the-round and I don't intend to run away, so I'm going back to the boarding house. You can find me either there or at the tent should you decide to press charges."

David stood and leaned over the table, supporting himself with his hands, glaring at Robyn. "Oh, no, you don't! I told you, you're going to stay here where I can keep an eye on you—"

Suddenly, Belinda broke into the conversation. "Wait a minute. What's this about pressing charges and running away?"

David brushed aside her question. "This is between Robyn and me, and—"

"I think you'd better tell her, David," Robyn said. "She has a right to know." She turned and looked at Belinda. "It was my car that hit Shelley," she said quietly.

For a moment Belinda looked blank. Then, as she realized what Robyn had said, her face became flushed with anger. "You!" she raged. "You hit my baby? Why, you little slut!" She turned to David. "What's she doing here in *my* house? Why isn't she in jail?"

David's attention had been diverted to Belinda. "All this doesn't concern you," he growled. "It's my responsibility, and I'll handle it."

"Doesn't concern me?" Belinda was practically screaming by now. "It was my daughter she hit, and you say it doesn't concern me? Well, if you won't have her put in jail, I will."

Belinda jumped out of her chair, only to be pushed back into it by an enraged David. "Sit down and shut up, dammit! If you were so concerned about Shelley, how come it took you a whole week to get here? I called you from the hospital as soon as we'd gotten her there. Don't waste your talent playing the noble mother scene for me. I'm not impressed."

Belinda was about to reply, then obviously thought better of it and made a great show of drinking her coffee. David then turned to Robyn. "As for you, I don't want to hear any more talk about your leaving. You'll stay here until I send you away. Is that understood?"

Robyn felt a twinge of fear at David's wrath, but she wasn't going to let him talk to her like that. She stood and faced him. "I'm not a child for you to order around!"

He pushed his face up close to hers and lowered his voice to an ominous rumble. "Maybe not, but I think you'd find it to your best advantage not to cross me, Robyn."

Robyn's eyes widened at the obvious threat of prosecution, and she stalked out of the room. As she left, she heard David speak to Graham. "I advise you to go home and make a pass at your wife if that's what you've got in mind, but leave Robyn alone, or I won't be responsible for the consequences!"

Once in her room, Robyn's exhaustion caught up with her, and she took a nap. She dreaded another scene with Belinda at lunch, but the actress was charming to everyone but Robyn, whom she ignored. It wasn't until Robyn mentioned rehearsals that she got Belinda's full attention. "You're an actress?" she said, the proper amount of astonishment in her voice to indicate that such a thing was too ludicrous to be considered.

"Not an actress," Robyn replied. "A performer. I'm in the chorus at the theater-in-the-round."

"The chorus?" drawled Belinda. "How quaint."

"That's where you started, so don't knock it," David reminded her.

Belinda smiled at him sweetly. "But darling, I studied theater arts in college."

Robyn smiled equally sweetly at Belinda. "How nice. I have a bachelor's degree in music, and I also studied drama."

After lunch, David, who was not on call at the pet hospital that weekend, told Robyn he'd take her to rehearsals. She said she'd take a bus and did. She wasn't going to let him dictate to her about everything.

Belinda had said she was spending the afternoon with her best friend and former neighbor, Eve Welles. Robyn could already feel the hatchet buried in her back. If Belinda had resented her before she talked to Eve, she was really going to hate her after she heard Eve's totally wrong version of the accident.

Sunday was dress rehearsal, and it was a long, hot, exhausting day. Everything went wrong. Francine Jordan, the television star who had been brought in to play the lead part of Laurie, complained of a sore throat and sang off key. Curly Russell, the country-western singer, who was making his first appearance in the area as Dusty, the male lead, showed up with a hangover, and Tyler Kerr, the highstrung director, alternately roared and sulked.

That was only the beginning. When they got into their costumes, Robyn's dress was three inches too long, one of the men dancers had boots a size too small and three of the long ruffled petticoats the girls wore under their calico dresses were missing altogether. To top it all off, the saxophone player collapsed and was sent home with a temperature of 102 degrees. Robyn wondered why she hadn't taken up a more relaxing profession, such as maybe transporting nitroglycerin over bumpy country roads.

When they were finally dismissed, she got a ride home with one of the cast members who was going that way. Irene was putting the finishing touches on dinner, and Robyn stopped to tell her that she wouldn't be coming down for the meal, that she was too tired to eat.

She took a hot, relaxing bath and donned a buttercup-yellow nightgown. She turned her radio to a station that played only soft, soothing music and brushed her thick, auburn hair until it gleamed in the pale lamplight before climbing into bed with a novel she hoped to finish before sleep caught up with her.

She'd just settled down when there was a light tap on her door. She assumed it was Shelley, whom she hadn't seen all day, and called, "Come in." The door opened, but it wasn't Shelley. It was David with a large tray of covered dishes of mouth-wateringly aromatic food.

He walked to the bed and put the tray over her lap as she watched with surprise. There was a look of concern on his face as he said, "You can't rehearse those strenuous dances all day in this heat and then not eat. I know you're exhausted, but once you've put away that bowl of vegetable soup and started on Irene's seafood casserole, you'll feel better."

She wondered if she'd ever understand this man who held her heart in the palm of his hands. How could he be so dictatorial one moment and so tender and considerate the next?

Robyn smiled wearily. "You didn't have to do this, David."

He pulled up an upholstered chair and sat by the side of her bed. "I know I didn't, but I wanted to. Do you mind if I have some coffee and talk to you while you eat? I haven't had a minute alone with you since Belinda came."

Of course, they hadn't had any time together. Belinda monopolized his time when he was home. Robyn thought he'd wanted it that way.

She poured coffee into the two cups on the tray and

handed him one. "Are you sure your wife won't mind?" she asked.

"She's not my wife anymore, and it doesn't matter whether she minds or not." David leaned forward in his chair. "Robyn, about the night she arrived. I'm sorry—"

He must have seen her wince because he hurried on. "Oh, not because of what we were doing. I'd finally gotten you in my arms again, and if she hadn't come in, I don't think I could have let you go, but the problem is that she did come in, unexpected and unannounced, and it was not only awkward but damned embarrassing for you. I'm sorry about that, sorry you were put through such a scene."

The delicate china cup he held in his big hands rattled ominously in its saucer, and he set it down on her tray. "Believe me," he pleaded. "I had no idea she was coming."

Emotion welled up in Robyn, and she gave up trying to eat her soup. He was actually apologizing to her! Somehow she'd never thought he would do that, never thought he'd feel the need to do it. She looked at him and smiled. "I know that, David. You were just as shocked as I was by her sudden appearance."

His gaze fastened on her as he said, "Then why are you so mad at me? Why do you refuse to come near me? Why wouldn't you even talk to me today?"

Robyn was too astonished to reply. Was it possible he didn't realize that she knew he was sleeping with Belinda? Or did he honestly believe that since they'd been married for nine years before the divorce, there was nothing wrong with bedding her when she was in town?

Well, maybe it was natural enough, especially if he was still in love with her, but did he really have so little respect for Robyn that he thought he could go from Belinda's bed to hers? Maybe he expected to alternate. Belinda's bed one night, Robyn's bed the next.

She was startled out of her reverie by David's voice, harsher than before. "Robyn, answer me. Now what have I said to upset you?"

She blinked and was about to speak when another knock on the door distracted her and Shelley's voice called, "Robyn, are you asleep? Can I come in?"

David sank back in the chair and swore softly as Robyn replied, "Of course you may, Shelley."

The door opened, and the child tottered in, clumsy in her unwieldy cast. She looked at David and smiled. "Hi, daddy, I didn't know you were up here with Robyn."

David picked her up and sat her on his lap. "Hi, baby. I brought Robyn her dinner, but I was just leaving."

He stayed on for a few minutes while Shelley told them both in great detail about the tricks she was trying to teach her new puppy, which she had named Cinderella; then he excused himself and left. Robyn felt a wave of regret. Maybe they could have found a common ground for settling their differences if they'd had a little more time alone. Still, it seemed highly unlikely. Much as she loved David, longed to be with him, she couldn't, wouldn't, share him with Belinda.

Monday morning was like all mornings before an opening night. The box office was predicting a sellout by curtain time, and the cast was keyed up—exuberant one moment, prophesying doom the next. The opening-night jitters was bad enough, but compounding it was the fact that it was the first day of rehearsals for next week's show. It wasn't all bad, however. Running through the new songs and trying to adapt to the intricate dance routines kept everyone's minds off the impending performance that evening.

Rehearsals broke early, and back at David's, Robyn took a leisurely bath, shampooed her hair and set it in big rollers that would give it bounce but not a tight curl. She manicured her fingernails while she sat under the portable hair drier, and by the time she'd finished, her hair was dry, and it was time to go back to the tent for makeup and last-minute costume adjustments.

Robyn had warned Irene in advance that she never ate dinner before a performance, but David and Belinda were in the living room having cocktails, and Shelley was watching television as they waited for the meal to be served. Robyn stopped in to say good-by, and Shelley hugged her and promised they would be in their seats early. Belinda smiled and in a patronizing tone murmured, "Break a leg," while Irene came from the kitchen to remind Robyn to take a sweater, since it would no doubt be chilly after the show.

David walked out to the driveway with her where Will waited with the Cadillac to drive her. David opened the door, but before he helped her into the car, he took her in his arms and murmured, "Don't be nervous, sweetheart. Your sparkle will light up the tent. Just remember, we'll all be out there in the audience cheering you on."

He kissed her then, and Robyn forgot everything but the warmth that stole over her as she melted against him. It took awhile before they managed to pull apart, and when they did, she touched her lips to the pulse that was hammering at the base of his throat. "Oh, David," she whispered. "I wish we'd met under different circumstances."

She pulled away quickly, before he could reply and got in the car. As they drove away, she felt that she could have floated perfectly well without the automobile. *Sweetheart.* He'd called her sweetheart! And he'd been as shaken by that kiss as she had. Was it possible that he felt something deeper for her than just a physical desire? Surely if all he wanted was sex, he didn't need her; he had Belinda.

Robyn was slammed back to earth with a painful jolt. There was the whole agonizing situation capsulized into three damning words. *He had Belinda!* All of his needs were taken care of for the present, and she wasn't going to let him keep her simmering on the back burner for future use when Belinda once again took off and left him.

The dressing rooms were in portable buildings set at the back of the lot that temporarily housed the huge tent, and they were alive with activity. Actors and actresses, singers and dancers, were applying makeup, wrestling with nineteenth-century costumes, and yelling for the hairdressers. Half of them had lost something, and the other half had something that didn't belong to them.

The excitement of an opening night! Robyn had found that it was always the same, whether they were opening a new show or the same show in a different town. The thrill caused the adrenalin to flow through her body, producing a high that no drug could duplicate.

The audience began arriving, slowly at first, then in

large groups, and finally came streaming through the gates, forming lines for service at the snack bars or just mingling on the paved courtyard in front of the tent. It was a sellout crowd, and Robyn knew that David, Belinda, Shelley, and Irene, were there as well as Graham and Eve. Joyce had been conspicuous by her absence since Belinda had arrived, and Robyn felt a sense of kinship with her. They had both been displaced by an expert.

Then the lights blinked, and the audience began filing into the tent and making their way to their reserved seats. The men who handled the lights climbed to their niches at the top of the tent, the stagehands checked the props they would carry onto the stage during the next change of scene, and the cast made last-minute touch ups on their makeup and hair.

Finally, Robyn heard the burst of applause as the members of the orchestra marched down the aisle and into the pit at one edge of the stage, then the first strains of the overture. The show had begun!

Two and a half hours later, as the rousing finale rocked to a close, the audience rose to its feet and gave the performers a thunderous standing ovation. As Robyn took bows with the rest of the chorus, she knew that her face was flushed not only from exertion but with excitement and the thrill of knowing that the show was a smashing success and she'd had a tiny part in making it so.

Back in the dressing rooms, pandemonium reigned with much hugging, kissing and back slapping as the cast again repaired their makeup. This time it was in preparation for their appearance at the opening-night party that would be given each Monday night in the outside courtyard. They'd been instructed not to change out of their costumes but to appear as they had on stage and mingle with the audience as they sipped punch or wine and munched fancy cookies. The press would be there, possibly even a television crew from Denver.

As she made her way through the crowded court-yard, Robyn was stopped repeatedly by fans who wanted to offer congratulations or ask for an auto-graph, so it was a few minutes before she spotted the Christophers and the Welleses. Shelley saw her at the same time and shouted and waved. Robyn hurried over, and Shelley hugged her around the waist and babbled excitedly about how great the show was. Irene's turn was next, and even Belinda held out her hand and commented about the high quality of the performance. Then she waved at someone in the crowd and announced, "Oh, there's Francine and Curly," referring to the two stars of the musical, and rushed off to greet them.

Graham hugged Robyn and kissed her lightly, then told her she was the prettiest lady in the cast. Eve frowned at Graham but admitted to Robyn that she'd enjoyed the performance.

Then Robyn was standing in front of David. She was suddenly shy as she looked up into his deep-green eyes. She saw approval there and something else, a sadness bordering on pain. He reached out and gathered her to him. She wound her arms around his neck and lifted her face for his kiss. It was gentle, unhurried, but with an undercurrent of leashed passion. She returned it eagerly, wishing it could go on forever.

So, apparently, did David because it wasn't until they were jostled by the crowd that he broke off the kiss and rubbed his cheek against hers. "I'm proud of you, my little shooting star," he murmured in her ear. "I'd give anything if you were in a different profession, but if you have the necessary dedication, you'll go far in show business." His arms tightened as though he couldn't hold her close enough, and his voice broke slightly as he said, "I want you to be happy, and if this is what you want, then I wish you every success."

They were totally unaware of the crowds that swirled around them, or of Shelley and Irene and the Welleses watching as Robyn's fingers caressed the back of David's blond head. "All I need to be happy is for you to hold me the way you're doing now," she answered honestly. "And if you'll kiss me now, I'll be even happier."

David caught his breath and stiffened, then held her away from him and looked at her. His face was unreadable, and she was afraid she'd offended him until he said, "If you mean that, then come home with me—now."

It was a command, not a request, but it didn't matter. She nodded. "All right, but it will take me about ten minutes to clean off my makeup and change clothes."

A look of relief swept over David's features, and his fingers dug into her waist. "You mean you're willing to leave all this"—he gestured toward the crowd, the news people, the cameras and microphones—"to come home and be with me?" It sounded more like an accusation than a question.

Robyn was startled, uncertain of what he wanted her to say. "Yes, of course. Didn't you know I would?" She tried to pull away. "If you've changed your mind, if you don't want to—"

He tugged her to him in a grip that almost took her breath away, and his voice was husky as he whispered, "Oh, Robyn, if I tried to tell you how much I want you, I'd make a fool of myself."

He kissed her again, quickly this time, then released her. "Go change your clothes. I'll let the others know that we're leaving."

Robyn was back in less than the ten minutes allotted, but she knew she'd sacrificed glamour for speed. The change of clothing she'd brought to wear to the late supper with the other members of the chorus was still packed in her small bag. Instead, she wore the wheat-colored jeans and matching shirt she'd worn to the tent earlier. A brown, green and yellow silk scarf knotted around her neck supplied the only color, and her face was devoid of makeup except for lipstick. A hasty glance in the mirror had told her that the excitement of the evening had left her with a rosy glow that needed nothing to enhance it.

David, Irene and Shelley were waiting where she had left them, and David was talking to another couple who moved away as she approached. David smiled at her and took her arm. "One thing about the theater," he teased. "It teaches you all about quick changes."

He started to lead her toward the gate, but she held back. "Where's Belinda? And how about Graham and Eve?"

David urged her on as Irene and Shelley walked beside them. "Graham and Eve came in their own car, and Belinda is right in her element."

He nodded across the courtyard, and Robyn saw the actress standing with the stars of the show, surrounded by reporters and admiring fans. Cameras clicked, and one of the local DJs pointed a microphone at Belinda as he asked her questions. It was obvious that she'd forgotten about David and her daughter.

Robyn looked at David, but his only expression was one of concentration as he maneuvered them through the crowd. She was puzzled. "But shouldn't we wait for Belinda?" she asked.

He shook his head. "I talked to her. She's going to a late dinner party with the leads. If I know Belinda, she won't be home until very late."

When they got home, Irene took Shelley upstairs to put her to bed, and David turned to Robyn. "Would you like to go out to eat? I just remembered that you didn't have any dinner."

She shook her head. "No, I'm really not very hungry. I'll just fix myself a sandwich."

She headed for the kitchen, and David followed her. "Do you want a sandwich, too?" she asked as she took sliced turkey breast, cheese, mayonnaise and butter from the refrigerator.

"No, thanks," he answered as he handed her a loaf of bread from the cupboard. "I'm going to fix myself a drink. What will you have?"

"No liquor, thanks," she said as she took two pieces of bread from the wrapper. "I'll have a glass of milk."

Her words seemed to trigger David's temper, and he glared at her. "You're not making any points with me by pretending you never touch alcohol, and I wish you'd stop it. I've never accused you of being an alcoholic, just of bad judgment in driving a car when you'd been drinking more than usual."

As Robyn braced herself against the stabbing pain, she wondered why she was always surprised by David's attacks. She endured the whiplash of his cutting words regularly, and each time she let her guard down, she was totally unprepared for it. Now he had banished the glow of the evening and left her feeling drained and unutterably weary.

She put down the knife she'd been using and turned away. "I've changed my mind. I'm not hungry, after all," she said, sounding tired and defeated. "I'm going to bed."

She'd only taken a few steps when there was a strangled sound behind her, and David caught her around the waist with both arms and held her to him. "Robyn, I'm sorry!"

She struggled, but his grip tightened, and he rubbed his cheek in her thick hair. "Don't fight me, please. Don't you know what you're doing to me? I'm being torn apart, and I can't stand much more of it."

Robyn stopped fighting him then, and he turned her around in his arms and cuddled her to him. She could feel his heart beating wildly against her and knew that he really had been upset when she'd tried to walk away. She lifted her head to look at him and caught her breath when she saw the naked anguish in his eyes.

She put her arms around his neck and caressed his cheek with hers. "Oh, David, if you'd only believe me—"

He pressed a finger against her lips. "No, we're not going to talk. We've done enough talking to last a lifetime, and all we do is fight. I don't want to quarrel with you anymore, Robyn. I want to love you."

With one arm still around her waist, he led her out of the kitchen, down the hall to the master bedroom suite. He was taking her to his bedroom, and with all her heart Robyn wanted to go there with him, to spend the night with him making love, but then what? There were so many unresolved problems in their relationship. Would he love her tonight and prosecute her tomorrow? She couldn't trust him, had no reason to trust him, and still—

She held back and said, "David, I don't think—"

He smiled at her. "My bedroom is large, sweetheart. We'll sit on the couch in front of the fireplace. You won't have to go near the bed unless you want to. I'm not going to force you to do anything."

No, he wouldn't force her. She knew that. She also knew that it wouldn't take force to get her into bed with him. All it would take were a few kind words and his caressing touch on her body.

It didn't seem to matter what her brain warned her of. Her legs had a mind of their own, and they carried her beside David into a huge, very masculine room. There was a low fire in the fireplace to ward off the late-night chill of the mountain air, and they sat on the chocolate-brown couch, wrapped in each other's arms.

David's kisses were like a potent drug drawing her deeper under their influence. They had been tender at first but then deepened and became more intimate as the fire in the fireplace waned and the fire in their bodies flamed. David unbuttoned her blouse, and his mouth followed his hands, taking possession of her soft white breasts and the rosy nipples that hardened rapidly under his touch.

Robyn's trembling fingers were clumsy as she wrestled with the buttons on his white silk dress shirt, and David chuckled as he came to her rescue, then groaned as her fingers played with the heavy thatch of blond hair on his chest and her lips teased along his collarbone. His hand gently kneaded her thigh, inching upward until she throbbed with need. Her fingers roamed up and down his spine, and his mouth claimed hers with a passion that was almost out of control.

David shuddered and lifted his head. "In another minute, I'm not going to be able to stop. We'd better move over onto the bed."

Robyn was too inflamed to resist, and it came as a surprise when she heard herself murmur against his ear, "Do you think there will be room there for the three of us?"

He quirked an eyebrow and grinned. "Three of us? Who were you planning to bring along?"

She moved restlessly under his probing hands. "I mean you and me and Belinda."

His hands stopped probing, and he sat up straight, bringing her with him. "What in hell are you suggesting?" he demanded.

Robyn pulled away from him. "I'm suggesting that since you and Belinda share the same bed, she's not likely to be pleased to find me there with you when she comes home."

The fire in David's eyes was a mixture of lingering passion and advancing rage. "Just what makes you think that Belinda and I are sleeping together?"

Robyn finally had her treacherous body under control, along with her emotions. "For heaven's sake, David, give me credit for a little intelligence," she exclaimed. "I've seen her go to your room at night and come out of it in the morning. Besides, she's made no secret of the fact that you still live together as man and wife when she's staying here." She was buttoning up her blouse with shaking fingers.

David stared at her for a minute as though incapable

of speech, then began to laugh. He thought it was funny! He was laughing at her!

She jumped up and started for the door, but he was too quick for her. Still laughing, he grabbed her by the arm and whirled her around to face him. "Robyn, you little idiot, is that what you've been mad at me about?"

Damn him! What made him think it was so hilarious? She tried to twist away from him, but he caught her shoulders in both his hands and held her still. The laughing had ceased, but he still sounded amused. "Sweetheart, listen to me. It's true that Belinda sleeps in this wing of the house, but she has her own room." He nodded toward a closed door. "Right there, on the other side of the bathroom. Here, let me show you."

He took her arm and led her to a door that opened onto a large bathroom, elegantly tiled in brown and beige. They crossed through it to another door that David opened to reveal a bedroom that could have belonged only to Belinda. It was furnished and decorated in the style of the movie queens of the past. Everything was white, from the thick carpet on the floor to the quilted silk on the walls. A portrait of Belinda, dressed in a slinky white gown, hung over the white-brick fireplace, and in the middle of the room, a massive round bed was covered with white satin. The only color in the room came from a vase of blood-red roses and green leaves.

Robyn drew a shuddering sigh of relief and leaned gratefully against David as he put his arm around her and led her back to his room. He kissed the top of her head and murmured, "Did you really think I was trying to seduce you and sleeping with Belinda all at the same time?"

Before she could answer, there was a tap on the door, and Belinda's honey tones called, "David, darling, open up. Why have you locked the door? I'm sorry if you're upset with me for staying out so late, but I promised to come to you the minute I got home, and here I am. Now be a doll and open the door, or would you rather I come in through my room and the bathroom. After all, that's the way we usually get back and forth, isn't it?"

Chapter Seven

David muttered an oath that turned the air blue as he bounded across the room and flung the door open with such force that it was nearly torn from its hinges. A startled Belinda stood framed in the doorway, looking gorgeous as usual in her mauve silk organza dress. Her eyes widened as she looked from a glowering David to a stunned and disheveled Robyn, and her voice was all innocent amazement when she said, "Oh, my, I do seem to always arrive at the wrong moment." Her gaze settled on David. "Darling, you didn't tell me you were going to be—entertaining."

Robyn's pride and theatrical training finally came to her rescue. She straightened her shoulders and sauntered toward Belinda. "Don't apologize. We were all through with our—entertainment." She gestured toward David. "He's all yours, but you may have to wait for him to get his batteries recharged. He's not as young as he used to be."

She strolled past Belinda and David and down

the hall toward the stairway. She didn't even turn around when David roared something unprintable and slammed the door.

The next morning Robyn managed to leave the house without seeing anyone. At the tent she was greeted by a jubilant cast whose main topic of conversation was the rave reviews in the morning newspapers. Tyler Kerr was especially impressed with the review in the Denver paper, and someone handed Robyn a copy as the director read aloud. It was flattering to both the cast and the unusual theater, but Robyn noticed that it was written by a man named Paul Vernon. She called to Tyler and asked, "Who is Paul Vernon? I thought Lowell St. James was the drama critic for this newspaper?"

Tyler grimaced. "He is, and he'd promised to be here last night, but he called and said something had come up and he couldn't make it. Paul Vernon is one of his promising protégés." He shrugged. "I'd hoped for the prestige of a St. James review, but at least this Vernon fellow liked the show."

At the bottom of the page, Robyn noticed a picture of Belinda with the stars of the show and a brief write-up noting that she was a former resident of Boulder, now a well-known actress, and visiting family in the area. Neither David nor Shelley were mentioned.

It was a long and difficult day, with the regular company trying to adjust to the two new stars who were taking the lead roles in the next performance. The man playing the hero was a fading Broadway actor with a drinking problem, and the woman playing the heroine was a health-food fanatic who kept telling the male lead he'd die young if he didn't give up liquor. He explained that it was too late for that since he was already past fifty and the only thing that he was allergic to was milk.

Robyn concentrated on her dancing and singing and pushed all thoughts of David and Belinda out of her mind. After rehearsal, she went with two of the other chorus members to their apartment for a light snack. Afterward, she went straight back to the tent. She knew she should have called Irene to let her know she wouldn't be home, but she had no desire to communicate with the Christopher family. If only she could find the man who was driving her car when it hit Shelley and prove that she was innocent. Then she could get away from David before he broke her heart.

That evening, they again played to a full house and once more received a standing ovation when the show was over. It looked as though Boulder was wholeheartedly enthusiastic about theater-in-the-round and would support the season.

Robyn took her time cleaning off her makeup and changing out of her costume and into her jeans and shirt. She was tired, but she didn't want to go home until she was reasonably sure David had gone to his room. She didn't want a scene with him, and she couldn't bear to watch him and Belinda go off to their suite together. Her mind told her she hated him until her body took over and reminded her how much she loved him.

She ran the brush through her auburn hair and applied a touch of lipstick, then threw a lightweight sweater around her shoulders and walked toward the door. She'd have to call for a cab because David still had her car keys. She hesitated to wear her contact lenses yet, but tomorrow she could pick up her new glasses, and then she'd demand her keys back.

Robyn stepped off the porch and started across the dimly lit grassy area between the dressing rooms and the tent when she heard someone call her name. She turned in the direction of the voice and saw a tall figure approaching her in the near darkness. She didn't have to wonder who it was even though she couldn't see him clearly. She seemed to have an invisible antenna that picked up the strong sensual vibes that radiated from David whenever he was anywhere near her.

He reached her in two giant strides and took her arm. Robyn pulled away from him and demanded, "What are you doing here?"

He walked alongside of her but made no move to touch her again. "I haven't seen you since you stormed out of my room. Did you really think I'd leave you to find your way home alone in the middle of the night, especially when you're so upset?"

"Upset?" she cried. "I'm not upset. I've never been more calm, and I hope you roast in hell."

His voice was grim. "I'm sure you do, and if what you're thinking was true, I'd deserve to do just that, but in spite of what she's led you to believe, I'm *not* sleeping with Belinda."

Robyn gasped at the audacity of his statement. Was it possible that he was telling the truth? Had Belinda been deliberately causing trouble? Her words had certainly been calculated to do just that. . . . No, it wasn't possible. Belinda couldn't have known that Robyn was in the locked room with David!

He took her arm again as they started across the street to the parking lot. She knew that this time she wouldn't be able to shake him off, so she didn't try. Her voice throbbed with unshed tears as she said, "David, don't lie to me. I don't care whether or not you're sleeping with Belinda. All I want is for you to leave me alone. I think it would be better if you did charge me with drunk driving. At least then I wouldn't have to live with your constant threats. I could leave your house, get away from you."

By now they had reached the car, and he unlocked the door and helped her inside, then went around and climbed into the driver's seat. Before he started the engine, he turned to her, his voice low, husky. "Is that what you really want, Robyn, to get away from me?"

No, it wasn't what she wanted, and the knowledge frightened her. Was there something wrong with her, a flaw in her character that made her cling to a man who despised her enough to torture her the way David did? There was a name for that kind of flaw. Masochism. She shuddered.

She sank back in her seat and looked away as he started the car. "Yes, David," she answered. "I do want to get away from you. There's something a little sick about our relationship, and I want out."

He drove out of the parking lot and headed home. "That's not true." He sighed. "We're two healthy adults with normal sexual appetites who are attracted to each other. I meant what I said, Robyn. I'm not sleeping with Belinda. I realize now that she's been lying to you, giving you a totally erroneous impression about our relationship. I haven't touched her since she's been here this time."

"But you have at other times since your separation." It was a statement, not a question.

"Yes," he admitted. "It took me a long time to come to terms with losing her. In the early years of our marriage, things were good between us. It was only after she started gaining recognition as an actress that it all began to fall apart. I wanted a wife, a mother for my child. I even wanted more children. All she wanted was a career."

She heard the bitterness in his tone. "It got to the point where I couldn't live with her, but I also had a hard time living without her. I didn't want to give up all those years of being together. I hoped we could iron out our differences. It wasn't until last year that I finally filed for divorce and custody of Shelley."

He was laying bare all his wounds, and Robyn ached for him. She'd known a number of couples, both friends of her parents and close personal friends, who had gone through the purgatory of divorce, and she had an idea of what David had been suffering. She wanted to comfort him, but the comfort he wanted was the forgetfulness of lovemaking, and that was something Robyn couldn't risk. She knew that if they ever made love, she would be hopelessly, totally enslaved by a man who only wanted a brief encounter.

They drove the rest of the way home in silence, and once there, David ushered her into the kitchen and insisted that she eat. Irene had fixed a plate of cold cuts, potato salad and a molded lime Jell-O and fruit salad and put it in the refrigerator for her. The coffee was hot in the electric coffee maker, and David warmed freshly baked yeast rolls in the microwave oven.

They sat at the kitchen table while she ate and David continued to talk. "I didn't follow after you last night and try to explain because I knew you were too upset to listen. Instead, I stayed there and dealt with Belinda."

He shifted angrily in his chair. "I could have killed her with my bare hands! I swear that until then I had no idea she was giving you such a bad time. I told her to pack her things and get out. She said if she did she'd take Shelley with her. She had me there. She has visiting rights, and she's allowed to have Shelley with her part of the time."

David's gaze met Robyn's, and she could see the hurt and frustration in his green eyes. "I couldn't let her take Shelley to a hotel, not now that Shelley needs special care, so I had to back down and allow Belinda to stay. She'll only be here a few more days. She has to be back in Hollywood soon."

Robyn put down her coffee cup and touched her lips with her napkin. "Of course you couldn't let Shelley go to a hotel with her mother. Besides, there's no need. This is Belinda's and Shelley's home. If anyone leaves, it will be me."

David's gesture was one of disagreement, dismissal, but Robyn plunged on. "It's past time for me to move into a place of my own, David. Shelley is fine—there will be no complications from her injuries—and surely you know by now that I'm going to stay here for the run of the musicals. I have no right to be here in your house, and I can't blame Belinda for resenting me. Let me go, please."

His chair scraped against the glistening linoleum as he pushed it back and stood. He paced around the kitchen as he spoke. "Let's get one thing straight. This is not Belinda's home. It's mine, mine and Shelley's. The only reason Belinda's here is because she's Shelley's mother and has visiting rights. You are not to let her intimidate you."

He stopped pacing and came to stand beside Robyn. "If you've finished eating, let's go someplace more comfortable."

He pulled out her chair, and she rose. "All right," she agreed, "but not the bedroom."

He grinned. "If you would just spend one night in bed with me, we could resolve all our differences very pleasurably."

He put his arm around her waist, but she pulled away. She was stung by his casual attitude and said so. "You really believe that, don't you, David? You think sex is a panacea for all disagreements between us. You say you want me, but you don't. You want a bed partner, and since I'm reasonably attractive and not unresponsive, you've decided I'm the one to best fill your needs. It doesn't matter what *I* want, what *I* need, what *my* moral standards are."

David threw her a murderous look and clamped his hand around her arm. "For heaven's sake," he sputtered, "if we're going to quarrel, let's do it in the den where we won't be overheard."

He marched her down the hall and into the cozy book-lined room where he seated her on the couch none too gently, then sat down beside her. She slid over to the other side, leaving a long cushion's length between them. The dim glow from the lamps would have been romantic under other circumstances.

"Now what's this nonsense you're spouting?" he demanded angrily. "You sound like someone's maiden aunt." He stopped and stared at her for a moment. "Good Lord, are you trying to tell me you're a virgin?"

Robyn could feel the hot color flood her face, and she stammered when she spoke. "I—I'm n—not t—trying to tell you anything about my sexual experience. That's none of your business. I'm me, Robyn Flannery, twenty-three years old and a college graduate. I'm a woman with wants and needs and a goal in life. I am not a sex object who falls into bed with every man who thinks he wants her."

"I've never thought that you were, and you know it," David snapped, "but what have you got against making love with a man who arouses you?"

She stood and walked away so she wouldn't have to face him. "Not a thing," she said softly. "Making love with a man you love, with a man who loves you, must be a beautiful experience, but you haven't once mentioned love, David, or marriage."

She heard him stand up and walk toward her; then his arms stole around her waist and pulled her back against him. She could feel the extent of his arousal, and she couldn't suppress a shiver of raw desire that shook her. "You know how much I care for you, Robyn," David said softly. "I'd have preferred charges against you for hitting Shelley as soon as we got back here if my feelings for you hadn't gotten in the way. Do you think I make a habit of blackmailing women to live with me? I couldn't let you get away from me."

His lips nuzzled her hair and the side of her throat while his hands slid up to stroke her breasts. She closed her eyes and leaned against him, and she knew he could feel the throbbing beat of her heart, which seemed to be pumping molten fire through her veins. Her hips, with a life of their own, gyrated slowly against him, and he groaned as his arms tightened and his teeth nibbled at her ear lobe.

"Stay with me, sweetheart," he murmured. "I'll be good to you, care for you, I promise. Romantic love is an emotional trap, and we don't need it. What we feel for each other is more sensible. I don't ever plan to marry again, and if I did, I would never marry another actress, but we can live together, express our feelings to the fullest, be friends as well as lovers."

He must have felt her stiffen because he hurried on.

"It's more sensible that way, Robyn. There are no strings in a relationship like that, no ties. When your engagement here is finished and you decide to move on either to television or the movies, the break can be clean, without the hassle and bitterness of a divorce."

Robyn bit her lip in an effort to hold back the scalding tears that brimmed in her blue eyes. It was odd. David had just shattered her hopes and her dreams, and she couldn't even be mad at him. He'd been hurt even more deeply than she'd realized by his selfish, heartless wife. Robyn could give him love, warmth, even more children, everything he needed so badly, but she could only do it in the context of marriage, a loving commitment, and that was the commitment he could not, would not, give her.

In spite of her effort, the hot tears poured down her cheeks. She straightened and pulled out of his embrace then, unwilling to let him see her cry. She walked away from him as she choked, "Good night, David."

The following morning was cloudy, with the smell of rain in the air, and Robyn was surprised to find Belinda already having breakfast in the dining room when she came downstairs. Belinda was not usually an early riser, and Robyn eyed her wonderingly before she decided to ignore the animosity between them and try to be pleasant. "Good morning, Belinda," she said as she sat down and poured herself a cup of coffee from the silver pot. "You're up and around early."

Belinda looked like an untouched maiden in her white satin nightgown and chiffon peignoir, but her mood was more that of an unpaid harlot. "How can you be so cheerful at this time of the morning? I've an appointment with Lowell St. James in a couple of hours, and it's going to take me that long just to wake up."

"Lowell St. James?" Robyn's eyebrows rose in surprise. "Is he coming here, or are you going to Denver?"

"He's coming here, of course," she snapped. "He saw the picture and write-up about me in yesterday's paper and called for an appointment."

Well pardon me, Your Highness, Robyn thought, but she was determined not to let this woman anger her again. Fortunately, Irene just then appeared with Robyn's breakfast and the information that Dr. David had an early call to the veterinary hospital and was already gone. The two women ate in silence.

It started to rain about nine-thirty that morning, but the orchestra drowned out the sound of water pelting the big tent as the chorus went through their song-and-dance routines. They broke at noon for lunch, and after that Robyn was free until the evening performance since Tyler was rehearsing only the speaking roles that afternoon.

She stopped at the oculist's to pick up her glasses before taking a bus home. It was good to have them again. She'd almost forgotten that the trees had individual leaves and that signs were painted sharp and clear rather than blurred and run together as she had been seeing them.

Robyn got off the bus at the stop nearest the Christopher home, and despite the light rain, climbed the three blocks to the stately redwood-and-brick residence. As she walked up the curving driveway, she was surprised to see a big red van with the logo and call letters of a Denver television station parked at the curb in front of the house. The back of the vehicle was open, and as she watched, two men came out the front door carrying what looked like cameras and bars of lights, and they stowed them in the van.

As she approached, she heard one man say to the other, "That's it, buddy. Let's be off. St. James has his own car. He can stay as long as he likes."

Robyn had forgotten the interview Belinda had scheduled with Lowell St. James. Belinda hadn't mentioned that it was a television profile, and Robyn had assumed it was to be an article for the Denver newspaper. She hastily rerouted her steps and walked around to the kitchen door on the south side of the house. She didn't want to intrude on Belinda's moment of glory with the Denver drama critic.

Robyn was greeted by a grumpy Irene, who muttered something about strangers tramping all over the house and making a lot of extra work as she loaded dirty dishes into the dishwasher. "I declare," she grumbled, "that Mrs. Christopher is the most inconsiderate woman I've ever worked for. I wish she'd go back to California and leave us alone."

Robyn decided this was one conversation she couldn't tactfully take part in, and she started to excuse herself to go up to her room when Shelley came bursting into the kitchen, her pale little face aglow with excitement. "Oh, Robyn, you should have been here. I was on television!"

Robyn hugged her and exclaimed, "How exciting, darling. My, you do look pretty. Is that a new outfit?"

The youngster was wearing wide-legged jade pants that fitted easily over her cast and accentuated the green in her sparkling eyes. With it she wore a color-coordinated print shirt and a scarf of the same material to hold back her mass of golden curls.

She's a lovely child, Robyn thought. Someday she'll grow up to look like her beautiful mother.

"Not really," Shelley answered Robyn's question. She took Robyn's hand and tugged at her. "Come in the living room and meet Mr. St. James. He was on television with mama, daddy and me."

Robyn allowed herself to be led to the living room. She tried hard to ignore the jealousy that was gnawing at her. David had been on television with Belinda and Shelley. Just one happy family, the famous actress, her handsome husband and their cute little daughter. Belinda was using David to enhance her public image, and worse, he let her. Didn't that prove that his feelings for her were deeper than he would admit?

Belinda, wearing a clinging turquoise outfit, was standing in front of the fireplace talking to David, who looked ruggedly handsome in a multicolored silk shirt and deep-brown slacks that fit tightly over his slender hips and well-shaped thighs. They glanced up as Shelley and Robyn came into the room. Shelley looked around, then asked, "Where's Mr. St. James? I brought Robyn to meet him."

Belinda's gaze hardened, but David smiled and said, "Robyn, I didn't know you were home. Hey, you finally got your glasses."

At the moment, Robyn's glasses were more of a hindrance than a help because they had been rained on during her walk from the bus stop and were spotted and streaked. She removed them and began to polish them with the bottom of her knit pullover blouse as Shelley repeated her question. "Daddy, where's Mr. St. James?"

"You mustn't pester Mr. St. James, Shelley," Belinda snapped. "He's too busy to meet all your friends, and I'm sure Robyn has something else to do."

Belinda had no intention of sharing her interview with Robyn, and that was fine with Robyn. She held up her glasses to look through them and said, "Your mother's right, honey. I'll just—"

A strangely familiar male voice from behind her cut her off. "Your man has brought my car around to the front, so I'll be leaving. It's been a real pleasure—"

That voice. Where had she heard that voice? Still gripping her glasses in her hand, she turned slowly to face the ordinary-looking man standing not more than three feet away from her. The medium-colored hair, medium-colored eyes and medium height could have belonged to at least a third of the men in Boulder, but they didn't. This particular combination of average features belonged to the man who had touched her life briefly and left it in shambles. He could be none other than the renowned drama critic, Lowell St. James.

He was also the man who had hit Shelley with Robyn's car and then run away!

Robyn's glasses slipped unnoticed to the floor as she stood rooted to the spot. Lowell St. James! My God, no wonder she hadn't been able to find him! He'd been to the cocktail party, after all, but once he'd escaped from the accident scene, he'd gone back to Denver and never again returned to the theater-in-the-round.

Lowell was looking at David as he spoke and for a moment or two didn't see Robyn. Then she heard David introducing her, and Lowell turned to her, a smile lighting his face as he offered his hand. "Miss Flannery, I'm pleased—"

He stopped in midsentence, and she knew he had

recognized her. The blood drained from his face, and a look of something akin to terror leapt into his eyes. The smile was frozen in place, like a picture trapped forever on film.

Robyn's voice sounded harsh, choppy, as though she was forcing the words through a raw throat. "You! You're the man who was driving my car. You're the man who hit Shelley and ran away! You—you—"

There was a lot of commotion going on around her, but Robyn's entire attention was focused on Lowell St. James, the drunken driver who had sped around the dangerous curves on an unfamiliar road in a blinding thunderstorm and hit David's small daughter, then fled the scene of the accident, leaving Robyn to take the blame. He stepped back as though afraid she was going to attack him, and she could see him struggling to regain his composure.

She turned to David and Belinda, who were standing in shocked silence, still unable to comprehend what was happening, and her words were coming more easily now as she said, "David, this is the man I told you about. This is the man who was driving my car that night and hit Shelley."

David snapped out of his trancelike state and wrapped his hand around Robyn's trembling arm. He looked perplexed, unbelieving. "Robyn, are you sure—"

. Lowell St. James broke in, his voice clear and unwavering. "My dear girl, I've no idea what you're talking about. I've never seen you before in my life."

Robyn stared at him and wondered if she looked as wild and out of control as she felt. Lowell St. James had made a remarkable comeback. He looked shaken ! in complete control and ready to use whatever means necessary to discredit her story. She told it, anyway, repeated again how the stranger, whom she now recognized as Lowell St. James, had asked her for a ride to his wife's sister's cabin in Boulder Canyon. How she had let him drive because she'd broken her glasses. How he'd been drunk and driving recklessly when he'd taken the wrong turn off the highway and hit Shelley and how he'd run away after pulling her unconscious form behind the steering wheel and fastening her in with the seat belt.

Lowell watched her with a look of utter amazement, and his calmness only drove Robyn to be more insistent in her accusations. Her hands itched to slap that smug look off his face, but she knew she was on the ragged edge of hysteria and a violent action of that kind would push her over. She didn't want that. She had to keep her senses about her somehow to prove to David that she was telling the truth.

When she'd finished her improbable story, Lowell spoke in a cool, rational voice. "I think we'd all better sit down. It's apt to take awhile to impress upon this child the folly of making wild accusations that have no substance in truth."

Robyn was trembling with fury and tried to deny his subtle insinuation that she was a pathological liar, but David led her to the couch and sat down beside her as the others took seats opposite them.

Lowell St. James spoke again. "Dr. Christopher, I assume this young woman is a member of your household?" David nodded, and Lowell continued. "Up until now, this problem seems to have been a family matter, but I cannot protest too strongly at having been dragged into this girl's fantasies."

"My accusations are not fantasies!" Robyn shouted,

and tried to stand, but David pulled her back down beside him and put his arm around her waist to hold her there.

"Sit still, Robyn, and be quiet," he said. "You've had your say. Now it's Mr. St. James's turn."

He kept his arm around her but spoke to Lowell. "Were you at the cocktail party that afternoon, Mr. St. James?"

Lowell reached into the pocket of his tweed sport coat and brought out a gold cigarette case. He opened it and extracted a cigarette before he answered. "Yes, as a matter of fact, I was. I'd arranged an interview with Stafford and Eden, the producers of those musicals." He searched his other pocket and brought out a lighter. "In fact, now that she's mentioned it, I remember talking to Miss Flannery briefly, but our conversation was not quite the way she described it."

He flicked open the lighter, lit his cigarette and inhaled deeply. "She bumped into me on the porch as she said, and during the course of her apology and my acceptance, I mentioned that my wife had dropped me off at the house and then gone on to visit with her sister and would be back any minute to pick me up." He closed the lighter and dropped it back in his pocket. "That's all there was to it. She left, and a few minutes later my wife arrived, and we drove back to my sister-in-law's cabin, where we spent the night."

The frustration in Robyn had built to the exploding point. "That's not true!" she cried. "You practically begged me to take you to the cabin. You said you had an important appointment in Denver that you couldn't miss!"

Lowell tapped his fingers on the arm of his chair and looked at David. "I hope you have enough control over this young woman to keep her from making these wild charges public, Dr. Christopher. I really cannot allow this type of thing to get around. I have a reputation to protect. Is she under the care of a psychiatrist?"

Belinda spoke for the first time. "Lowell, I can't tell you how sorry I am. I told David he should press charges against this little drunk and let the authorities handle it, but he's always been a sucker for a pretty face." She turned to glare at David. "I hope this has taught you to quit dragging strays home with you."

Everyone had forgotten about Shelley until she stood and addressed her mother, her little face tight with anger. "Robyn's not a 'drunk' and a 'stray.' She's nice. She took care of me when I was hurt. She cares about me."

The child started to cry, and Robyn twisted away from David's restraining embrace and jumped up, her own anger forgotten in her concern for David's daughter. She went to Shelley and put her arms around her. "Shelley, baby, it's all right. We'll get it all straightened out." She started to move across the room, taking the youngster with her. "Why don't you go upstairs and play with Cinderella? I'll ask Irene to bring you a glass of milk and some of those peanut-butter cookies she baked last night."

Shelley wiped her eyes as they stopped at the bottom of the stairway. "Can she bring Cinderella a doggy treat, too?"

Robyn tousled the blond curls. "Sure, I'll tell her. Run along now."

Shelley trudged reluctantly up the stairs, and Robyn walked past the other startled adults in the room and headed for the kitchen. She was glad for the interruption. She needed a breather, a chance to think.

By the time she'd delivered her message to Irene and returned to the living room, she'd calmed down and was once more thinking clearly. David, Belinda and Lowell were deeply engrossed in conversation, but they ceased talking when Robyn entered the room. She stood a little away from them and said, "There are two other people involved in what happened that night." She looked directly at David. "I want you to talk to Mrs. St. James and her sister. Mr. St. James must have arrived at the cabin that night late and soaking wet, possibly even injured. They can corroborate at least the last part of my story."

David looked at Lowell, who was sitting calmly, but it seemed to Robyn that he had winced slightly at her suggestion. "Robyn has a point, Lowell," he said. "Do you have any objection to me questioning your wife and sister-in-law?"

Lowell shifted. "As a matter of fact, I do," he said quietly. "I don't like the idea of them being upset by this tall tale, but if you insist, I'll call and tell them we're coming. They're both at the cabin."

"No!" Robyn was emphatic. "Don't let him use the telephone, David. He'll warn them, tell them what to say."

David looked from Robyn to Lowell. "I think that's a reasonable request. Will it inconvenience your family too much if we just drop in on them?"

A flash of anger crossed Lowell's face as he stood, but his voice was steady. "Of course it will be inconvenient, but since you seem determined to give this—this girl the benefit of the doubt, we might as well get it over with. I'll lead the way, and you can follow in your car."

They drove in silence, David and Belinda in front and Robyn in back. Belinda had started to rail at

Robyn as soon as they got into the car, but David told her bluntly to shut up, and she did. When Lowell turned across the highway and onto an access road, David told Robyn that the road to his summer home was the next one up. A short distance up the road, Lowell drove into the driveway of an A-frame home that, like David's, could hardly be called a cabin. It was nestled back among the giant trees, again like David's, and there was a redwood deck across the front.

Lowell St. James opened the front door and called, "Erma, Kate," as he led them into a huge space that was living room, dining room and kitchen, separated by low room dividers. The two women answered his call, one from a chair in front of the fireplace and the other from the kitchen area. When they saw that Lowell had guests with him, they hurried to the center of the room where he introduced them as "Erma, my wife, and Kate Jensen, my sister-in-law."

The confused women invited them to sit down and offered drinks, which everyone refused. Then Lowell took the floor and started to talk. "This young lady"— he looked at Robyn—"Miss Flannery, has made some very serious accusations against me, and she seems to think that you two"—he motioned to his wife and sister-in-law—"can back them up."

Robyn had been watching the two women closely. There was a strong family resemblance. Both were slender, medium height and rather mousy looking. They were definitely not the assertive type. Erma St. James blanched when her husband made his statement, and Kate Jensen looked frightened. *I was right,* Robyn thought with rising excitement. *They do know what Lowell St. James did that night. I knew it!*

St. James continued, this time speaking directly to his

wife. He seemed calm, relaxed, but his eyes bored into hers as though trying to send her a message. "Erma, do you remember that day about two weeks ago when we drove to Nederland where I was doing an interview with the producers of the theater-in-the-round? You dropped me off at that restored Victorian mansion and then came on here to visit with Kate."

Erma seemed to draw into herself as she nodded but didn't speak.

"Okay," St. James continued, "now tell these people"—his hand swept in the direction of Robyn, David and Belinda—"what happened after you left me there."

Erma looked at them and blinked. "Well," she began timidly, "I drove here to Kate's cabin, and we visited for an hour or so. Lowell had asked me to pick him up at six-thirty, so I left here about six-fifteen. He was waiting for me on the sidewalk when I got there, and we came back here. It was storming pretty bad, so we spent the night here with Kate and went back to Denver the next morning."

Robyn gasped and jumped to her feet. "You're lying!" she shouted. "You know he was gone when you got there!"

"Miss Flannery!" Lowell's voice had the cutting edge of a knife. "I will not tolerate you berating my wife! You were the one who insisted on questioning her. Now either be quiet and listen to what she has to say or leave."

David was on his feet, too, and his hold on Robyn's arm was not gentle as he muttered, "Robyn, sit down. And I'm warning you, no more outbursts!"

Robyn had no choice but to sit back down. She knew she was harming her cause rather than helping it by her fiery displays, but the woman was lying, and she couldn't be allowed to get away with it.

David, still on his feet, asked the next question, directing it at Kate Jensen. "Mrs. Jensen, do you agree with your sister's statement? Did they come right back here together and spend the night?"

It seemed to Robyn that the woman hesitated a second too long, but then she spoke in a quiet, even voice. "Yes, Dr. Christopher, they did. Erma and Lowell were back here within half an hour after she left to pick him up. I urged them not to try to drive back to Denver in the storm, so they spent the night here with me. They didn't leave the cabin at all until the next morning."

Robyn could feel the panic building with every word spoken. She was being railroaded, framed, set up—whatever the term, it was a terrifying experience. These nice-looking, soft-spoken, upper-middle-class people were lying through their teeth, and there didn't seem to be anything she could do about it. These two women were protecting Lowell St. James from a very nasty charge of drunken hit-and-run driving. His reputation and probably his career would be ruined if the truth were known, and his wife and her sister weren't about to let that happen no matter who was hurt by their silence.

Robyn was trembling with frustration and fear. What could she say now to make David believe her? How could she clear herself of the charge of reckless drunken driving when the only three people who knew the truth had no intentions of telling it?

She wound her arms tightly around herself to try to still the shivering that racked her. From what seemed like a distance, she heard David say, "I'm sorry, Mr.

St. James, that you've been put through this. I've begged Robyn to tell me the truth of what happened, but from the beginning she's insisted there was a stranger, a man, driving her car that night and that he disappeared afterward. She seems incapable of facing the fact that she hit Shelley."

Lowell looked at Robyn with contempt. "Why should she, Dr. Christopher? After all, she's an actress, and a good one. She had you almost believing her, and it was your child she hit. I'm warning you, though, if these unfounded allegations are ever made public, I'll sue, and I'll sue you because you're harboring her!"

Chapter Eight

The short trip back to Boulder seemed to take forever, as Robyn curled up in the back seat of the luxurious Cadillac and tried to shut out the sound of David and Belinda quarreling in the front.

Belinda was furious, not only at Robyn but at David for not having Robyn "locked up" where she belonged instead of bringing her home to "my house." David told her it was his house, his responsibility, and he'd done what he thought best. The battle was off and running.

This was apparently an old argument, and Robyn was merely the latest catalyst. Belinda accused David of deliberately trying to ruin her career, her life, everything she'd worked so hard to achieve. David retaliated with a scathing indictment of her performance as a wife and mother and told her she'd never cared for anybody but herself and her blasted career.

Robyn was too wrapped up in her own misery to spare much concern for the two raging people in the front seat. Lowell St. James had coldly and deliberately lied. Not only that, but he had somehow managed to convince his wife and sister-in-law to corroborate that lie. It was too pat, too well rehearsed to be spontaneous. They must have thought it all out in advance.

Well, why was she surprised? She would very likely do the same thing for David if he were ever in trouble. Love had few moral standards when the beloved was threatened with disaster. Only now she was the one facing disgrace, and she knew that David would no longer protect her. Why should he? She'd brought him nothing but unhappiness, dissension and pain—and he didn't love her.

When they finally got home, Belinda and Robyn got out of the car, and David drove it around to the garage. Without a word, Belinda stalked into the house, leaving Robyn to follow behind. She heard a door slam in the direction of the master bedroom suite and knew Belinda had gone to her room.

Robyn had just started up the stairs when David came in and called to her. She turned to look at him and was dismayed to see how white and drawn he was. His mouth was set in a grim, hard line, and the turmoil he was feeling was evident in his green eyes. "I want to talk to you," he said curtly. "Please come into the den."

He walked away, and she followed, dreading the scene she knew was to come.

It had stopped raining, but the sky was still overcast with heavy gray clouds, giving the book-lined den a cheerless, depressing air.

David closed the door and leaned wearily against it as Robyn walked to the center of the room, bracing herself for his tirade. It wasn't long in coming. "Robyn, how could you?" he said in a deceptively soft voice. "I've done everything in my power to help you even though it was my own daughter you injured. I could have turned you over to the police; I've actually broken the law by not doing so. I've protected you, sheltered you, even against my better judgment I've grown to care for you, and you repay me by not only lying about a mysterious stranger but actually accusing a prominent man of the crime."

He moved away from the door and began to prowl around the room as Robyn stood with hands clasped and head bowed, accepting his judgment, knowing there was nothing she could say to prevent or delay it.

David spoke again. "You've ruined Belinda's television profile, embarrassed me and upset Shelley. You're a walking disaster. You leave a trail of destruction wherever you go. It wouldn't be quite so unforgivable if you showed some remorse, but you don't."

"I've nothing to be remorseful for!" Robyn blurted out, unable to endure his false accusations any longer. "I did *not* hit Shelley! Everything I've told you is the truth. It's Lowell St. James who's lying!"

David hit his palm with his fist, swearing. "You can be thankful I'm not a violent man!" he shouted. "I've never been so tempted to hit a woman before in my life!"

He turned and headed for the door, flung it open and started down the hall with Robyn in pursuit. "David, where are you going?" He jerked open the front door without answering, and Robyn ran to catch up. "David, don't take the car. You're too upset to drive!"

He headed around the house toward the garage as he called over his shoulder. "I've had a bellyful of deceitful women. I'm going to my club to get smashed, and please spare me your tender concern!"

*   *   *

A short time later, when dinner was announced, Robyn forced herself to sit at the table and eat with Shelley even though the food curdled in her stomach. Belinda was still shut up in her room with no apparent concern for her tearful daughter, who badly needed someone to soothe away the fears the quarreling and violence of the afternoon had stirred in her.

After dinner, Robyn played video games with Shelley and later put her to bed and read to her. By the time Robyn kissed the child good night and tucked her in, Shelley was calm and once more at peace.

Not so Robyn. She paced up and down her room, her mind a cauldron of tormented, disjointed thoughts. She no longer had any hope that she could make David believe the truth of what happened the night of the accident. Lowell St. James and his women had seen to that. There really wasn't any reason for David to believe her; all the evidence was against her. St. James was an honorable man, a pillar of the community, a celebrity, whereas she was an actress, a transient show-business performer, never in one place more than a few weeks at a time. She had no permanent address, no ties to any community, no character references.

She went to the closet and took down her scruffy, well-traveled blue luggage and opened it on the bed. This time there was no question but that she must leave, and she doubted that David would try to stop her. She had brought him and his family nothing but sorrow and pain.

Robyn began folding clothes and putting them in the suitcases. St. James had admitted just enough of the truth to make his story believable, and she knew there was no way she could prove that he was lying. Her love for David was as deep as ever, but it was a love that had been doomed even before it was born.

She finished her packing, soaked for a long time in a tub of warm, fragrant bubble bath and crawled into bed where she lay wide-eyed and miserable until morning.

She overslept again and realized she'd forgotten to set her alarm. She dressed hurriedly in a black leotard over which she buttoned a red wrap-around skirt and ran downstairs, all the time praying that David hadn't left yet. She had to see him to get the keys to her car and tell him she was moving out.

He wasn't in the living room or dining room, and Robyn was afraid she'd missed him until she pushed open the kitchen door and saw him sitting at the round oak table, his head in his hands. He was dressed in scruffy jeans and a T-shirt. He looked up when she came into the room, then groaned and dropped his head back in his hands, but not before Robyn had seen his white face, red-rimmed eyes and the stubble of unshaven beard.

Her pulse quickened with alarm. "David, are you ill?" she asked, unable to keep the fear out of her voice even though he'd told her he didn't want her concern.

He raised his head again and rubbed his bloodshot eyes. "You better believe I am," he grumbled. "I never could drink much. It makes me sick instead of drunk."

A wave of relief and sympathy washed over her. He may feel miserable, but it was something he'd get over. She longed to reach out to him, to hold his head against her breast and soothe the pounding ache she knew he was enduring, but it was too late for that. The best thing she could do for both him and herself was get out of there quickly.

"I'm sorry you're not feeling well," she said. "Maybe you'd better go back to bed. But first please give me my car keys. I have new glasses now, and I want my car back."

He eyed her warily and muttered, "Later. Will can drive you one more day."

Robyn tapped her foot and held out her hand. "Now, David. I see just fine with my glasses, and may I remind you that *I'm* not the one who's hung over and unfit to drive."

He winced and stood as he put his hand in his pocket. "Okay, you've made your point," he grated as he produced the keys and dropped them into her upturned palm.

She was instantly contrite. After all, it was her fault he was in this condition, and the sooner she broke off all ties with him, the better. She took a deep breath and said, "I've packed my things and will be back to pick them up after rehearsal. I never meant to cause you so much grief."

He clutched the back of the chair he'd been sitting on as though to steady himself. "Where will you go?" His voice was dry, raspy.

She shook her head. "I'm not sure. Back to the boarding house if there's still room for me. If not, I'll go to a hotel until I can find a place. I won't run away. You can always get in touch with me at the tent if you decide to prosecute me for the accident."

David turned away. "I'm not going to prosecute you," he growled, and jammed his hands in his pockets. "You're free to do whatever you want. Maybe it's best that you do leave before we destroy each other."

A sob rose in Robyn's throat as she turned on her heel and ran out of the house.

There were still a lot of bugs to work out of the following week's production, and it was midafternoon before rehearsal broke up. Robyn had just enough time to pick up her luggage at the Christophers' and to take it to the boarding house before going back to the tent for the evening performance. She'd checked with her former roommate and found that she was still welcome to share the room.

She let herself in David's front door with her key, making a mental note to give it to Irene when she left. She counted on David's not being home this early. She didn't think she could face a polite, drawn-out good-by, but luck wasn't with her. As she walked through the spacious entry and into the living room, she saw him sprawled in his big leather recliner chair with his eyes closed.

She paused, then walked cautiously across the Oriental rug toward the staircase. She'd gone only a few steps when his voice, low and masculine, called her name. She stopped and looked back. His eyes were open now and boring into her.

Why, oh, why, couldn't anything ever be easy for her? Why did she have to do everything the hard way? How could she be calm and collected when her heart was breaking?

David continued to look at her, as though trying to memorize her. She didn't have to memorize him. Every time she closed her eyes, there he was, big as life and twice as desirable. Dear heaven, was she never to be rid of him?

Robyn had to do something to break the silence and

that penetrating gaze, so she said, "I didn't mean to wake you. How do you feel?"

He straightened up and yawned. "Like miniature bombs are exploding in my head and stomach. I want to talk to you, Robyn."

She backed away. "No. There's been too much talk already. We'd only hurt each other more." She looked at her watch. "I haven't much time. I'll just go up and get my bags and say good-by to Shelley. Is she home?"

He nodded as he stood. "I'll help you with the suitcases." He started toward the stairs.

"Oh, no, David." The dismay she felt sounded in her voice. "I can manage okay."

He paid no attention but continued up the steps, and she was left with no choice but to follow. Her luggage was stacked neatly in a corner of her pretty blue bedroom, the room she had come to think of as her own. She'd miss the elegant furnishings, the spaciousness and the view of the colorful gardens below.

She walked around, opening and closing drawers and doors, telling herself she was making sure she hadn't left anything but knowing that she wanted to touch once more the familiar items. The ache in her was overwhelming. What a stupid little fool she'd been to come here in the first place. She should have called David's bluff, let him drag her off to the police station if he'd wanted to. Graham had told her there wasn't enough evidence to charge her, and she knew he was right. She also knew that it wasn't fear of being arrested that had kept her here. It was an almost desperate need to be near David. David Christopher, the one man who could never love her!

He had been watching her, then abruptly picked up her luggage and asked if that was everything. She nodded, afraid to speak, and followed him back down the hall. They were halfway down the stairs when Shelley came bounding into the living room. She caught sight of them and stopped abruptly. "Daddy, where are you going? You didn't say you were going away."

David reached the bottom of the stairs and set the bags down. "I'm not, baby," he said. "These suitcases are Robyn's."

Shelley looked at Robyn with disbelief. "Robyn, are you going away?"

Oh, no, Robyn thought. She knew that if Shelley put up a fuss, she would break down, and that's the last thing she wanted. She forced what she hoped was a bright smile as she said, "Yes, I am, honey. It's time I went back to my own home."

"But you don't have a home!" the child wailed. "Daddy said you didn't."

Robyn twisted her fingers together and tried to keep her voice from breaking. "I have a room, Shelley, at the boarding house. That's my home for now. It's not as big and pretty as yours, but it's where I belong. I don't belong here, honey."

"Yes, you do!" Shelley cried as she flung her arms around Robyn's waist. "I want you to live here with us. Daddy'll let you stay, won't you, daddy?"

David said nothing, and Robyn held the small golden head against her. "Shelley, you know I can't live here. I'm not a member of the family. You have your daddy and your mommy and Irene. You don't need me. I have to live my own life."

Shelley raised her pinched little face, and tears ran down her cheeks. "That's what mama said when she left us. I thought you liked me. I thought—"

A shuddering sob cut off her words, and Robyn

couldn't stand it any longer. She sank to her knees and cradled the distraught youngster as her own tears mingled with Shelley's. "Oh, sweetheart! Baby, don't cry. I do care about you. I love you."

They rocked back and forth, clinging together and sobbing as David stood by watching, making no move to interfere. Finally, Robyn got her runaway emotions under control and murmured to Shelley as she stroked her curls. "I've got to go now, honey. I'm a working girl, remember?"

Shelley disentangled herself from Robyn and stepped back. "Will—will you come to see me?"

Robyn took a tissue from the pocket of her skirt and wiped the small wet face. "Of course we'll get together," she said, knowing she would never come to this house again. "Maybe your daddy will let you come to the tent some morning and watch rehearsals."

Robyn stood, then leaned over to give Shelley a hug and a kiss. "Good-by, baby. Remember I love you."

She was blinded by tears as she started across the room and didn't see David move directly in front of her. She ran into him, and his arms quickly enfolded her as she put her head against his hard, familiar chest and sobbed. He buried his face in her soft auburn hair and murmured, "Robyn. Oh, God, Robyn, don't."

It was all there in his voice, his desire for her, his need, his anguish, and Robyn felt a small sense of victory. David would let her stay, would probably do almost anything to get her to stay. Anything but marry her. He wanted her badly, and she wanted him, but she knew that if she lived here with him, it would be as his mistress, and she wasn't willing to sacrifice her self-respect even for David.

Neither was she willing to cheapen herself in Shelley's eyes. Even though the child was only eight, she'd know what was going on, and if she didn't, her friends and classmates would tell her. Children were wise beyond their years these days, and Robyn would not be that kind of role model for the little girl she loved so dearly.

David held her close, and she could feel the tension in him. Without even meaning to, she had messed up his life almost as much as Belinda had. If only she could break through the wall of distrust he had built between them, but that was impossible. She'd tried and failed. There were just too many strikes against her.

Robyn lifted her face and looked at him with tear-dimmed eyes. He bent his head, and his lips touched hers, then touched them again, and again before finally taking complete possession. Her mouth parted eagerly, and she clasped her arms around his neck as she melted into his urgent embrace.

It was Shelley's voice, filled with hope, that brought Robyn back to her senses. "Daddy," the little girl said, "you won't let Robyn leave, will you?"

Robyn turned her face, breaking off the kiss, and leaned back. This was madness! She had to get out of there—now!

She pulled away from David, picked up the nearest suitcase and fled. She'd send someone after the rest of her luggage later. She heard David calling her name as she slammed the heavy front door and ran to her car.

The next few days went by in a haze of pain and loneliness. Robyn hadn't fully realized how deeply she had been assimilated into the Christopher household. Shelley and Irene had become very dear to her, and she missed them. Especially Shelley, whom she'd come to love almost as a daughter. Robyn found herself listening for the child's joyous laughter, for her shouts of excitement as she played with her puppy. Every time Robyn got in her car to drive herself somewhere, she thought of Will Otto and his taciturn patience as he drove her to and from the tent in the Cadillac. Heaven help her, she even missed Belinda. At least life was never dull when Belinda was around!

And David. She couldn't think of David yet. During the day and evening, she was too busy to dwell on her unhappiness, but after the first night, when she'd alternately sobbed and paced the floor, she took pity on her roommate and forced herself to lie quietly in her lonely bed until sleep eventually took pity on her.

On Sunday, the show started at seven o'clock, an hour earlier than the other nights, and there were a lot of children in the audience. Robyn liked to play to youngsters—they were always so wildly enthusiastic. It was the last performance of the first musical in the series. Tomorrow would be the opening night of the second; then there were seven more weeks before she could leave Boulder and all her heartaches.

She'd been invited to attend a late buffet dinner at the home of one of the local members of the chorus after the performance. But as Robyn creamed off her makeup and dressed in the swing-skirted yellow dress she'd brought for the occasion, she knew she wasn't going. It was too much effort to keep up the cheerful façade a party required. She wondered if she'd ever again be really happy.

Robyn saw him as she walked across the grassy area to the lighted courtyard, empty now except for some of the crew members still locking up—and David. He stood to one side, looking like a blond male model in his impeccably tailored three-piece suit, and she knew he was watching for her.

Why didn't he leave her alone? Surely these emotional scenes were no more pleasant for him than they were for her. Why didn't he stay away and give her a chance to piece her life back together again?

She started to turn away, to cut across the back of the large lot and approach her car from a different direction, but then she paused. That would just delay the inevitable. If David wanted to see her, he could always find her. She squared her shoulders and walked over to him.

He saw her coming and moved toward her. He looked tired, and Robyn wondered if he'd had as much trouble sleeping as she had. They met in the middle of the courtyard, and he reached out as though to take her arm, then dropped his arm to his side and said, "Hello, Robyn. I've come to take you home."

She knew without asking that he meant his home, the home she'd come to think of as hers until so recently. Wouldn't he ever give up and accept the fact that she was not going to become his mistress, his playmate, to use and toss away when he found a newer, fresher one?

She shook her head. "No, David. We have nothing to say to each other."

He looked at her with a brooding thoughtfulness. "I have something to say to you, but not here. Please come with me. I promise I won't touch you unless you want me to."

She wanted to go with him; with all her heart she wanted one more chance to make him believe her, but she knew it would only prolong the agony. "No," she whispered, then cleared her throat and started again. "We—we've been all through this. Belinda—"

"Belinda's gone," he said flatly. "She left the same day you did. That was part of the bargain we made. She wanted Shelley and me to appear on television with her, and I agreed on the condition that she leave, go back to Hollywood and get out of my life. She was getting bored in Boulder, anyway. She always does after a few days."

"Oh, poor Shelley," Robyn murmured, her heart aching for the little girl whose mother was so uncaring.

David nodded. "Yes, poor Shelley, but it's you she cries for, not Belinda."

Robyn winced at the anguish his remark caused. He could have spared her that. He knew how she loved Shelley, how hard it had been for her to leave the child.

She turned and started to walk away, and this time he did take her arm as he walked beside her. His touch was like a blast of heat that melted her firm resolve, but with one last desperate effort to break the spell he always wove around her, she pleaded, "Please, David, I don't want to go with you."

He stopped and put his fingers under her chin to lift her face to his. "Yes, you do, Robyn," he said softly. "You're too sweet and loving to deliberately make me suffer like this. Let's go home and try to work through the problems that are tormenting both of us."

For the first time since she'd moved out of David's house, Robyn felt relaxed and secure as she snuggled into the posh upholstery of the long, smooth Cadillac. It frightened her that just being close to David could make such a difference in the quality of her life. What an idiot she'd been to fall in love with him, but she really hadn't had any choice. It had happened without her knowledge or consent.

David parked the car in front of the house and

helped her out. Inside, the night lights were on, but the downstairs was deserted. Irene and Shelley were in bed. David led her down the hall to the den where, he said, there was more privacy and no chance of unexpected visitors. He locked the door as he said it and seated Robyn on the white leather couch.

He didn't sit with her but hunkered down in front of the fireplace and took his time laying the fire. His back was to her, and he spoke as he worked. "I made a mistake letting you leave here, Robyn, but I've made so many mistakes in the past few weeks that one more is hardly surprising."

Robyn started to protest, but he hurried on. "I was still hoping rather frantically that what I felt for you was only physical desire that would eventually recede." He shook his head, still not looking at her. "I guess I was willing to go to any lengths, no matter how absurd, to protect myself from falling in love with another actress." He paused as he lit the fire. "The last few years of my marriage to Belinda were one long purgatory, and I swore I'd never go through anything like it again. Then I discovered that purgatory is nothing like the hell I've lived in since you left me."

Robyn gasped as his words seemed to hover in the quiet room. What was he leading up to? It sounded almost as if—No, that was impossible. He'd already told her he'd never fall in love again.

David stood slowly and faced Robyn for the first time. He looked stricken, uncertain, almost frightened. Frightened? No, never. David Christopher was never afraid of anything. He knew exactly what he was doing all the time.

So why was he standing there looking at her as though he expected her to punish him in some way?

Without quite realizing what she was doing, Robyn rose and started toward him. "David?" She stopped only a few feet from him. "I don't understand. What . . ."

He didn't touch her, but his eyes never left her face. "I know I'm botching it badly, Robyn, but I'm trying to ask you to marry me. In fact, I'm pleading with you to marry me."

Robyn blinked and stared at David, sure that her fantasies had taken over and deprived her of her reason. "You—you want to marry me?" she stammered.

He nodded.

"But—but why? You don't even like me."

He reached out to her then and stroked a wayward auburn curl off her smooth cheek. "I like you very much, my little songbird, and I love you to distraction." His fingers became entangled in her soft, thick hair and pulled her head back so that her face was close to his. "I want to marry you because quite honestly I can't function worth a damn without you. I can't eat, I can't sleep, I can't think. I even have to let my associates at the hospital do all the surgery because my hands aren't steady enough."

She looked at him, wide-eyed with surprise as he gently pulled her closer so that their lips were almost touching. "You're making an emotional wreck of me, sweetheart." His voice was little more than a whisper. "Won't you marry me and put me out of my misery?"

She blinked again, and the tip of her tongue licked her dry lips. "Oh, yes, David," she breathed. "Oh, darling, yes."

His arms circled her waist and molded her against him as their lips, so tantalizingly close, came together and clung. Her arms stole around his neck, and her mouth parted with a sigh of relief as her body melted into his. David's hands roamed over her back and pressed against her hips, making her intimately aware of how quickly she had aroused him. The muscles in the lower part of her stomach knotted in response and sent waves of heat pulsating through her.

After a while, David raised his head and murmured, "I was so afraid I'd lost you, that you'd never forgive me for my incredible stupidity. Robyn, darling, I love you so much, but for a long time I couldn't admit it, didn't dare admit it, even to myself."

She put her fingers to his mouth and he kissed them. "I know. You think I was drunk and plowed into Shelley with my car. I've never blamed you for that— the evidence was so incriminating—but I didn't do it. Oh, sweetheart, if there was only some way I could prove it—"

"No, Robyn." He broke into her sentence. "I know you're telling the truth about that. I think I've known it almost from the beginning, but I didn't *want* to believe you."

"Didn't *want* to believe me?" Robyn repeated, puzzled.

David began to loosen his tie. "Look, why don't we sit down and be comfortable? There's so much I want to explain to you. Do you mind if I take off my coat?"

She shook her head and smiled. "Of course not. Here, let me help you."

She unfastened his coat and vest as he pulled off the tie and undid the top button of his shirt. He shrugged out of the coat and vest and tossed them over a chair, then settled himself on the couch and pulled her down beside him. She snuggled against him and raised her face for another kiss, which was administered promptly and lingeringly. David stroked her high, round breasts, and Robyn wondered if he could feel the fast, erratic pounding of her heart as her fingers caressed the smooth, compact muscles of his shoulders.

His lips moved to the sensitive hollow at the side of her throat, and her arms tightened around him as she shivered with pleasure. "I love you, David," she whispered. "I've always loved you, right from the beginning when you carried me from the car into the house after the accident."

David lifted his head to look down at her, and she was sure she saw relief in his dark-green eyes. "Do you? I don't see how you could have anything but contempt for me. I've been such a bas—"

She put her hand over his mouth to stop the ugly word. "No, that's not true. You had good reason to distrust me." Then she remembered what he'd said earlier and asked, "David, what did you mean when you said you didn't *want* to believe me?"

He took her hand from his mouth and held it against his chest as he said, "Honey, I'd just ended a marriage with an actress, and the experience left me pretty bloody and beaten. No way was I going to get involved with another woman in show business. It was a matter of self-preservation, and I felt very strongly about it."

He cuddled her closer. "Then you came along. At first, I was too concerned about Shelley to do anything but vent my rage on you, but that first night when you came wandering into Shelley's room in that revealing nightgown of Joyce's—"

"How did you know it was Joyce's nightgown?" Robyn couldn't hold back the jealous question.

David grinned and rubbed the tip of her nose with his

own. "That, my love, is none of your business. Whatever happened between Joyce and me was before I met you. All that matters is that I haven't seen the garment since you wore it."

She buried her face in the side of his neck. "Did I look as enticing in it as Joyce did?"

"You looked like some of the small animals I treat, battered and bruised and pathetic, and you were so gentle and sweet with Shelley. I didn't like the feelings you were arousing in me, and I overreacted and was nasty to you. Instead of giving me the tongue-lashing I deserved and storming out of the room, you offered to sit with Shelley so I could get some sleep. You said I needed rest!"

His voice was soft, unbelieving, as he continued. "It had been such a long time since a woman had shown anything like tender concern for me that it damn near undid me. First I accused you of trying to seduce me, and then, when you looked like I'd hit you, I had an overwhelming desire to hold you, protect you, love you. I didn't even try to resist the urge, and when I did touch you, hold you, I was lost."

You could have fooled me, Robyn thought as she looked up questioningly. He nodded. "I know, I behaved like a beast, but I didn't want another woman to become important to me. I fought my feelings by lashing out at you, trying to make you confess that you'd been drinking and hit Shelley. But even then I knew you were probably telling the truth. I was sure of it after our walk in the woods when I kissed you and you responded so satisfyingly."

"You mean like this?" she asked impishly, and planted her lips firmly on his. Her tongue darted in and out of his mouth, and with a muffled groan, his hand crept up under her full yellow skirt and caressed her bare thigh, sending shock waves upward to already sensitized areas. As the kiss deepened, his wandering hand moved to the elastic band of her silky panties and started to pull them down. Robyn shivered with desire and knew if she didn't stop him now, she'd be past caring about anything but his full possession of her. She wanted that more than anything, but first there were still misunderstandings to be explained.

She tore her mouth from his and gasped. "David, please wait, just a little while."

His hand stilled and lay against her rounded derriere, and for the first time she realized he was trembling. For a minute, he didn't speak, then he murmured softly, "Be careful what you start, sweetheart. My self-control is severely limited. I may not be able to stop next time."

Robyn stroked his cheek. "I'm sorry. I don't mean to tease. I want you as much as you want me, but let's get all our problems straightened out first. I don't want either of us to have any reservations when we finally do—uh—"

David chuckled at her embarrassment over a choice of words. "Neither do I, but we'd better not take too long. I'm only human, after all."

"So am I," she assured him, "but I want to know why you changed your mind about believing my version of the accident."

He removed his hand from under her dress and cupped her breast, then laughed. "My God, there's no place I can touch you that doesn't set me on fire." He again moved his hand, this time to her waist. "Now, what was the question? Oh, yes. I changed my mind because less than an hour later I learned that you were an actress."

She tried to protest that she was a performer, not an actress, but he didn't give her a chance. "You can't imagine what it did to me when you announced so casually that you made your living singing and dancing in musical productions. That was the one occupation I simply couldn't tolerate in a new love. It was easy to tell myself that since you were an actress, you were also an accomplished liar who would hit a child and then lie about it to save your own skin."

He closed his eyes and hugged her to him. "I would have believed anything that would help me fight against the love I was determined not to feel for you."

For a minute they clung to each other, savoring the current of intense feeling that flowed between them. Then David relaxed his hold on her a little and sighed. "It was a hopeless battle, lost before it began, but I tried. Oh, how I tried! I even let you leave, although it was like having the heart ripped out of me, but all that proved was that I couldn't live without you. Our separation did accomplish one thing, though. I was forced to face a few facts, and I came up with two conclusions."

He stopped and Robyn, her curiosity aroused, prodded him. "Yes, what were they?"

He nuzzled her jaw line with little nibbling kisses that left a trail of flames. "First, I love you so desperately that I'll never again let you get away from me, and that leads to the second resolution."

He held her away so he could look at her. "Robyn, I'm not going to make the mistakes I made the first time. I won't ask you to give up your career. I've thought it over carefully. When the theater-in-the-round is over in the fall, if you receive an offer that takes you away from Boulder, I'll sell my practice, and Shelley and I will go with you."

Robyn jerked upright, too astonished to speak. It had never occurred to her that this man, who had defied his father and been partially disinherited in order to study veterinary medicine, would give up his profession for her. Tears of gratitude for his gesture gathered in her eyes as he turned her to him. He misunderstood and spoke quickly to reassure her. "It's all right, love. I have plenty of money. I don't need to work to support us."

The tears spilled down her cheeks and mingled with her wide smile as she took his head in her hands and kissed him. "Oh, David, my precious sweetheart, there's something I've tried to tell you all along, but you wouldn't listen. I'm not an actress, darling. I'm a teacher! I'm trained to teach music. The only reason I'm in show business is because I wanted a change from classrooms for a while. I'd been in school since I was five years old, and I intend to go back for my master's degree, but I was offered a part in the chorus of a touring company, and I took it. It was a lark, a break from studying, a chance to get a little firsthand experience so I could advise my future students on the joys and the pitfalls of show business."

David stared at her, ashen and uncomprehending. When he finally spoke, his voice was unsteady. "Why— why didn't you tell me?"

She took his hands in hers and kissed them. "I didn't think it would make any difference. I thought you hated me because you thought I'd hit Shelley and then lied.

Oh, darling, all I want is your love and maybe a couple of babies. I want to be a wife to you, a mother to Shelley, and to teach at the university."

With a groan that seemed to be torn from deep within him, David reached for her and enclosed her in his arms. He rained kisses over her wet face before attacking her mouth with a hunger that could not be tamed. Robyn held him tightly and arched her body against his as his hand once again found its way under her skirt to her bare leg and started to work its way upward.

With trembling fingers, she unbuttoned his shirt and ran her hands through the blond hair on his broad chest. Neither of them paid any attention to the chime of the doorbell as it pealed through the room. It chimed a second time, and Robyn stirred. "David, I think that was the doorbell."

If he heard, he had no intention of being distracted. He found the zipper at the back of her dress and started to lower it. The chime rang a third time, and Robyn pushed away from him. "Darling, there's someone at the door."

David heard it that time and swore. "Let it ring," he growled. "I'll be damned if I'm going to let anybody interrupt us this time."

The doorbell pealed again, and Robyn jumped up and reached behind her to zip her dress. "David, that noise is going to waken Irene and Shelley. Besides, it must be important. It's late for anyone to be visiting."

David muttered a most ungentlemanly oath and stood. "All right," he gritted, "I'll answer it, but I'm going to send them packing, and I'm not going to be nice about it."

He reached for his suit coat and put it on as he strode

down the hall with Robyn right behind him. He jerked open the door and thundered, "Do you have to make so much racket—"

He stopped abruptly, and Robyn peeked around him to see a well-dressed middle-aged woman standing in the porch light. She blinked and looked again. It was Kate Jensen, Lowell St. James's sister-in-law!

David held the door open and stepped aside. "Mrs. Jensen," he said. "I'm sorry. Please, come in."

Kate stepped inside and looked from David to Robyn. "I'm sorry to disturb you so late, Dr. Christopher," she said in a timorous voice. "I attended the performance at the theater-in-the-round this evening, and I was afraid if I didn't come now, tonight, I'd lose my nerve again and maybe not come at all."

David murmured something polite and led Kate into the living room where he turned up the lights and seated her in a wing-backed chair. Robyn followed, and he motioned her to the couch, then sat down beside her. "Now, Mrs. Jensen," he said, "I gather you want to speak to me. Do you mind if Robyn stays?"

Kate shook her head. "Not at all. I want her to hear this, too." She clasped and unclasped her purse, then grasped it with both hands as though clutching a life line. "I—I've always been an honest, law-abiding person and—and I just can't live with a lie any longer."

Robyn gasped. David took her hand and signaled her to be quiet as Kate looked at them. "I have a daughter about your age, Robyn, and all I can think of is how I'd feel if anyone did to her what Lowell, Erma and I are doing to you."

She covered her face with her hands. "I couldn't bear it, and I'm not going to be a part of this—this stupid conspiracy any longer."

David's voice was gentle as he said, "Kate, suppose you tell us exactly what happened the night Lowell came to your cabin late and dripping wet in the storm."

Kate looked up, surprised. "You know?"

He nodded. "I know Robyn is telling the truth, so Lowell had to have walked from my house to yours in that storm."

Kate sank back in the chair. "Yes, he did. It's true that Erma was late picking him up in Nederland and he was gone when she got there. My brother-in-law is a bully, Dr. Christopher, and Erma was afraid he'd be in one of his rages. She came back here, and it was a couple of hours before he showed up, soaking wet and badly shaken. He—he had a glass of whiskey and took a hot bath; then he started in on Erma."

Kate clutched the arms of the chair, and her voice was grim. "Lowell cursed my sister and slapped her. I—I tried to intervene, and he cursed me, too. He told us about the accident, that he'd hit a little girl and then arranged it so it would look like the woman who owned the car was driving. He ran away then and walked through the woods to my place.

"He was drinking as he talked, and he blamed Erma, said if she'd picked him up on time, none of it would have happened. We were afraid of him, and when he told us what we were to say if anyone ever questioned us about the accident, we didn't dare object. My sister will do anything he tells her to, and much to my lasting shame, I agreed in order to protect Erma."

Kate shifted to look directly at Robyn. "The whole thing was too unreal to bother me much until I saw you the other day. Since then, the desperation in your eyes and voice has haunted me until I had to see you again. I went to the musical tonight and watched you perform.

You're a lovely, talented girl, and I'm not going to be a part of ruining your future."

She stood then, and David and Robyn rose, also. Kate's voice was firm now as she said, "If it comes to a court action, I'll testify. I'll tell the truth about what really happened. I think my sister and I have been under Lowell St. James's iron rule long enough."

David and Robyn thanked Kate, and David escorted her to her car. Robyn wandered back to the den and sat down on the couch in front of the fire. It was burning low now, a warm light flickering in the darkness.

For the first time since the accident, Robyn felt truly at peace. The truth had finally been told, and never again would there be doubt about who had hit Shelley. The relief was enormous, but the most beautiful part of all was that David had believed her before she'd been exonerated by Kate Jensen. He had asked her to marry him on the strength of his love for her and his faith in her honesty even though all the evidence pointed against her. She knew there could be no higher proof of his love.

She didn't hear him return until he entered the room. She held out her arms, and he sank down beside her and cradled her to him. She put her head on his chest and murmured, "I couldn't help feeling sorry for her."

David stroked her hair. "I'm afraid I'm not quite so forgiving," he muttered. "Her silence put us both through weeks of torment."

"Are you going to report Lowell St. James to the authorities?"

He hesitated a moment, then answered. "No. Shelley will be all right, and I don't want a lot of publicity, but I'll let St. James stew about it. Maybe he'll learn a lesson."

David reached once more for her zipper and lowered it slowly as he whispered, "Now, let's see. Where were we before we were so rudely interrupted?"

Robyn giggled and raised her eager face for his kiss, a kiss that she intended to be repeated at close intervals during all the years of their lives.

IT'S YOUR OWN SPECIAL TIME

Contemporary romances for today's women.
Each month, six very special love stories will be yours
from SILHOUETTE. Look for them wherever books are sold
or order now from the coupon below.

$1.50 each

☐ 5 Goforth	☐ 28 Hampson	☐ 54 Beckman	☐ 83 Halston
☐ 6 Stanford	☐ 29 Wildman	☐ 55 LaDame	☐ 84 Vitek
☐ 7 Lewis	☐ 30 Dixon	☐ 56 Trent	☐ 85 John
☐ 8 Beckman	☐ 32 Michaels	☐ 57 John	☐ 86 Adams
☐ 9 Wilson	☐ 33 Vitek	☐ 58 Stanford	☐ 87 Michaels
☐ 10 Caine	☐ 34 John	☐ 59 Vernon	☐ 88 Stanford
☐ 11 Vernon	☐ 35 Stanford	☐ 60 Hill	☐ 89 James
☐ 17 John	☐ 38 Browning	☐ 61 Michaels	☐ 90 Major
☐ 19 Thornton	☐ 39 Sinclair	☐ 62 Halston	☐ 92 McKay
☐ 20 Fulford	☐ 46 Stanford	☐ 63 Brent	☐ 93 Browning
☐ 22 Stephens	☐ 47 Vitek	☐ 71 Ripy	☐ 94 Hampson
☐ 23 Edwards	☐ 48 Wildman	☐ 73 Browning	☐ 95 Wisdom
☐ 24 Healy	☐ 49 Wisdom	☐ 76 Hardy	☐ 96 Beckman
☐ 25 Stanford	☐ 50 Scott	☐ 78 Oliver	☐ 97 Clay
☐ 26 Hastings	☐ 52 Hampson	☐ 81 Roberts	☐ 98 St. George
☐ 27 Hampson	☐ 53 Browning	☐ 82 Dailey	☐ 99 Camp

$1.75 each

☐ 100 Stanford	☐ 114 Michaels	☐ 128 Hampson	☐ 143 Roberts
☐ 101 Hardy	☐ 115 John	☐ 129 Converse	☐ 144 Goforth
☐ 102 Hastings	☐ 116 Lindley	☐ 130 Hardy	☐ 145 Hope
☐ 103 Cork	☐ 117 Scott	☐ 131 Stanford	☐ 146 Michaels
☐ 104 Vitek	☐ 118 Dailey	☐ 132 Wisdom	☐ 147 Hampson
☐ 105 Eden	☐ 119 Hampson	☐ 133 Rowe	☐ 148 Cork
☐ 106 Dailey	☐ 120 Carroll	☐ 134 Charles	☐ 149 Saunders
☐ 107 Bright	☐ 121 Langan	☐ 135 Logan	☐ 150 Major
☐ 108 Hampson	☐ 122 Scofield	☐ 136 Hampson	☐ 151 Hampson
☐ 109 Vernon	☐ 123 Sinclair	☐ 137 Hunter	☐ 152 Halston
☐ 110 Trent	☐ 124 Beckman	☐ 138 Wilson	☐ 153 Dailey
☐ 111 South	☐ 125 Bright	☐ 139 Vitek	☐ 154 Beckman
☐ 112 Stanford	☐ 126 St. George	☐ 140 Erskine	☐ 155 Hampson
☐ 113 Browning	☐ 127 Roberts	☐ 142 Browning	☐ 156 Sawyer

READERS' COMMENTS ON SILHOUETTE ROMANCES:

"I would like to congratulate you on the most wonderful books I've had the pleasure of reading. They are a tremendous joy to those of us who have yet to meet the man of our dreams. From reading your books I quite truly believe that he will some-day appear before me like a prince!"

—L.L.*, Hollandale, MS

"Your books are great, wholesome fiction, always with an upbeat, happy ending. Thank you."

—M.D., Massena, NY

"My boyfriend always teases me about Silhouette Books. He asks me, how's my love life and natu-rally I say terrific, but I tell him that there is always room for a little more romance from Sil-houette."

—F.N., Ontario, Canada

"I would like to sincerely express my gratitude to you and your staff for bringing the pleasure of your publications to my attention. Your books are well written, mature and very contemporary."

—D.D., Staten Island, NY

*names available on request